MAYBE YOU KNOW A WOMAN LIKE CARA

She always attracted men, by her beauty or her quiet charm. She often attracted women—even children. For one reason or another she was loved, it seemed, by all around her—until her mysterious death revealed the hidden emotions below the surface of the town in which she lived.

Maybe you know a woman like Cara —but you'll learn much more about her in this revealing novel of a woman as destructive as she was charming— until she was destroyed herself.

SIGNET Books You'll Want to Read

☐ **MR. AND MRS. BO JO JONES by Ann Head.** A deeply moving story of two courageous teenagers caught in a marriage of necessity.
(#Y6440—$1.25)

☐ **ALWAYS IN AUGUST by Ann Head.** A spellbinding novel of romance and jealousy, violence and strange vengeance that will haunt you long after its last enthralling page. (#Y6023—$1.25)

☐ **FAIR WITH RAIN by Ann Head.** A wonderfully warm and entertaining novel about a delightful South Carolina family you'll wish were yours. "Recommended . . . a pleasant and shrewdly observed family, you can't help liking them." —**Chicago Sunday Tribune** (#Q5526—95¢)

☐ **HARRIET SAID by Beryl Bainbridge.** An explosive shocker about little girls . . . here is the horror of child's play mixed with erotic manipulation and evil possession. "A highly plotted horror tale that ranks with the celebrated thrillers of corrupt childhood."—**New York Times Book Review**
(#W6058—$1.50)

☐ **NEITHER THE SEA NOR THE SAND by Gordon Honeycomb.** In a story full of strange, enthralling horror about a young couple madly and possessively in love with each other, Gordon Honeycomb explores the darker ranges of human emotion—between the poles of love and death.
(#Q5283—95¢)

THE NEW AMERICAN LIBRARY, INC.,
P.O. Box 999, Bergenfield, New Jersey 07621

Please send me the SIGNET BOOKS I have checked above. I am enclosing $_____(check or money order—no currency or C.O.D.'s). Please include the list price plus 25¢ a copy to cover handling and mailing costs. (Prices and numbers are subject to change without notice.)

Name_____

Address_____

City_____ State_____ Zip Code_____

Allow at least 3 weeks for delivery

Everybody Adored Cara

By

Ann Head

A SIGNET BOOK
NEW AMERICAN LIBRARY
TIMES MIRROR

All the characters in this book are fictitious, and any
resemblance to actual persons, living or dead,
is purely coincidental.

COPYRIGHT © 1963 BY ANN HEAD MORSE

All rights reserved. For information address
The Estate of Ann Head, c/o Blanche C. Gregory, Inc.,
2 Tudor City Place, New York, New York 10017.

Library of Congress Catalog Card Number: 63-9180

This is an authorized reprint of a hardcover edition
published by Doubleday & Company, Inc.

SIGNET TRADEMARK REG. U.S. PAT. OFF. AND FOREIGN COUNTRIES
REGISTERED TRADEMARK—MARCA REGISTRADA
HECHO EN CHICAGO, U.S.A.

SIGNET, SIGNET CLASSICS, MENTOR, PLUME AND MERIDIAN BOOKS
are published by The New American Library, Inc.,
1301 Avenue of the Americas, New York, New York 10019.

FIRST PRINTING, MARCH, 1975

1 2 3 4 5 6 7 8 9

PRINTED IN THE UNITED STATES OF AMERICA

NEXT DOOR THE MAID, receiving no answer to her knock, was opening the door of Cara Sumner's blue and ivory bedroom, was carrying a breakfast tray to Cara Sumner's bedside, was saying, "It's a lovely day, Mrs. Sumner, and your favorite muffins," was waiting for Cara to open her eyes, to sit up, which she did not do and would never do again, for the maid was on the point of discovering that Cara Sumner lay dead in her bed, lay strangled with the chiffon scarf she had used to wear about her head when she drove the little foreign car that had no top.

A lawn, a hedge, a garden away, in the Merrill dining room, her friend Lindsey Merrill serenely poured her second cup of coffee.

"A lovely day," she murmured, letting her gaze wander out of the window and up to the very top of the maple tree where green leaves made a slowly shifting pattern against a light blue sky. "A lovely day for primroses," she said to no one in particular. The phrase, one she remembered from childhood, had popped into her mind from out of nowhere. Though she could no longer remember its origin, its meaning was still clear to her, recalling other days whose color, texture, and effect on her defied any more coherent description.

"A lovely day for what, my dear?" Frank Merrill, having finished with the business section of the paper, put it down and glanced impatiently at his son who, oblivious of his father's glance, showed no sign of relinquishing the sports page.

"A lovely day for the meeting of the Stoningham library committee, a lovely day for putting away winter clothes and letting down summer hems . . ." She sighed, "I don't suppose you'd consider letting the firm of Sumner and Merrill plow ahead on its own for a day and let me pack a picnic hamper, and . . ."

"You know that's absurd. Especially with Garfield out of town." Frank, though he spoke to his wife, still eyed the paper in his son's hands with mounting annoyance. Suddenly he reached across the table and flicked at the pages with thumb and forefinger. "How many times must I tell you that *you* have all day to read the paper while I . . ."

"Sorry," Johnny flushed, a habit he had of late whenever his father reprimanded him. He folded the sheets together, and with a snap of his wrist, handed them over. The gesture, had it not been for the smile that accompanied it, would have been insolent. His father, observing both gesture and smile, hesitated for a moment trying to decide. The smile, to Lindsey's relief, must have taken precedent, for he said nothing. She must, she decided, have a talk with Johnny about his attitude toward his father. Or was it perhaps Frank's attitude toward Johnny that . . . But could she really expect to bring two such opposites closer? Especially when one was so much older and held, when all was said and done, the whip hand. And how important was it that father and son understand each other? Did it really matter to anyone except herself, caught between them, weak and vacillating and burdened with love?

"If I do the dishes when I come back, can I go now?" Cathy was saying. "Can I?" Blue eyes made ludicrously large and knowing with whatever it was she painted in at the corners, beseeched permission. Lindsey found something intensely touching about Cathy these days . . .

Cathy trying to leap the gap from adolescence to young womanhood with the aid of eye shadow and a hairdo that looked like nothing so much as a night's restless tossing pinned to the top of her head . . . Cathy bubbling over with inarguable assertions about life, love, and the fate of civilization.

"Can you go where?" Lindsey toyed with a second roll, remembered the new size-twelve dress, and put it down.

"First to Bibsy's. Have you forgotten this is the day we're going job hunting?" Light and breathless, as though "this is the day we're going to the beach," "the day we're going to play tennis . . ."

"Are you sure you're serious about this?" Lindsey said. "A job isn't something you can take or leave depending on your mood."

"Don't worry, Mom," Johnny said. "They'll never get one. Not in a million years."

"And where do you plan to begin?" Frank regarded his daughter indulgently over the rim of the sports page. "With Stone's department store?"

"We thought we'd start there." Cathy pushed back her chair.

"And work on down to Brock's five and dime?" Johnny grinned.

"Well, if we have to." Her smile wavered, but only for a moment. "Anyhow, it isn't *where* we work that matters."

"I know, I know," Johnny said. "It's getting out from under and seeing the great big ugly world in all its penny-pinching, dollar-saving splendor."

"How old do you have to be to get a job at the dime store?" Marny queried pensively. Marny was eight and her skin and hair and eyes were all the same shade of brown. "How old do you have to be to run the popcorn machine?"

"Old enough to have outgrown an uncontrollable appetite for popcorn," her father said.

"Wish me luck," Cathy turned in the doorway, but it wasn't her parents' blessing she sought. She was looking directly at Johnny. Lindsey hoped he wouldn't let her down. Her need of his approval was a part of this transitional stage . . . the yardstick by which she measured her effect on the world of men.

"Good luck," he said, and grinned and made his fingers into a V.

Next door the maid was telephoning the doctor, any doctor, and the ambulance, and then riffling through all the scribbled notations on the pad beside Cara Sumner's bed . . . *Library meeting 11:00 . . . Call cleaners . . .* looking for the hotel in Chicago where Mr. Sumner was staying. But if Cara Sumner knew, she'd not written it down, at least not here. All of a sudden the maid realized she was alone in a room with death, and so she ran out of the room and down the stairs to the kitchen and sobbed to the cook that Mrs. Sumner, God rest her soul, was dead.

As soon as Cathy closed the screened door behind her, she began practicing how she would walk. She walked high in her black and white spectator pumps, holding her stomach in and her neck tall. "No, Mr. X, I've not had any experience, but I do know something about clothes and I like people." Passing the Sumners' house she was tempted to run in for a minute and ask Cara's advice about what to say and what not to say. Before she married Garfield, Cara had worked in New York and would know. That was the reason Cathy gave to the impulse. Actually she wanted to share her excitement, and Cara was the one person she felt would understand it. All of it. Johnny was wrong as wrong. There was much more to it than he guessed. There was Catherine Merrill with her own life to live. Her own world to make. Her own self to be. Though Cara was almost as old as her mother, Cathy never thought of her as her mother's contemporary. And it had nothing to do with their looks. Her mother, Cathy conceded, if anything looked younger than Cara except when Cara was really dressed up. No, it had to do with a kind of restless, seeking innocence that made Cathy think of her as much nearer her own age. It was almost as though in some intangible and incomprehensible way she, Cathy, and her mother's friend, a married woman almost twice her age, wrestled with the same problems. Though what Cara Sumner's problems could be she could not imagine. She simply accepted this curious affinity without attempting to probe it. Hesitating still, she saw that upstairs the curtains in Cara's bedroom swung aimlessly in the open window. She was, Cathy decided, still asleep.

Bibsy was waiting impatiently in the swing on the Michaels' front porch. Bibsy was small and dark and neat and cared so much about how she looked and what people thought it sometimes got between them. Like not liking the same music.

As soon as she saw Cathy, Bibsy leaped up scowling. "Don't you know how late it is? I thought we planned to be there when the doors opened. This town is just crawling with kids looking for summer jobs. I thought you *realized*."

Though she was two months and three days older, Bibsy always made her feel the younger. A little of the excitement, the anticipation, oozed away. Uncertainty took its place. "Do you think we've got a chance?"

"How on earth should I know?" Bibsy said, impatience making her sound cross, and silently Cathy fell into step beside her.

Johnny had known ever since that bit about the sports page that as soon as Cathy left the old man was going to get into him. He was so sure of this that as soon as he heard the door slam shut behind her, he tried to get away.

"Well, off to the salt mines," he said, and half rose out of his chair. But it was the wrong thing to say. The worst. The "salt mines" he referred to was his room where the first ten pages of the first act of the first play he'd ever tried to write lay on his desk screaming for his return. That's what the salt mines were, and his father knew it.

"Just a minute," his father said, and he could feel himself tensing up. "I didn't want to embarrass you in front of your more ambitious sister," he said, "but just what are *your* summer plans?" He pulled a pipe from his pocket and began slowly, patiently to pack it.

If only, Johnny thought, he'd find some other damned thing to do when he's about to get into me. Anything to vary the routine, he thought furiously, and said, "You know what my plans are. I've told you. The play . . ."

"I didn't ask you what you intend to do in your spare time."

"If it's money you're worried about, there's that four hundred Aunt Alma . . ."

"You know damned well it's not the money." Carefully his father brought the lighted match against the pipe bowl. "It's character I'm worried about. Yours."

"Marny, dear," his mother said, "if you'll get on your bathing suit, Cara said she'd keep an eye on you if you wanted to swim in their pool this morning."

"I'd much rather hear about Johnny's character," Marny said.

"Run along," her mother said, as though she'd not heard. "And be sure to let Cara know you're there so she can keep an eye out."

"I can swim as good as she can," Marny said, but she went.

"I don't expect you to believe it," Johnny said, "but it takes plenty of character to write a play, to finish it. Maybe more than I've got. But I want to know. I want to find out."

"Of course, of course," his father said with edgy reasonableness. "I'm sure it takes character of a sort, but it's not a thing that should take your entire summer. You can write any time. Nights. Sundays. When you get back to college. How do you think our best writers got there? You can write any time, but when but in summer can you get outdoors? Do a man's work and make a man's pay . . . learn the strength that comes with being your own man!"

"I am my own man," Johnny said. "Or trying to be."

"Darling," Lindsey said nervously, "perhaps there is some compromise. Part-time work . . ." She didn't know whose side she was on, but she rather thought this time it was Johnny's. There was more to growing up than getting to be a man. There was . . .

"But Mother, I thought I explained about that. I'm shooting for the Baxter award, remember, and there's a deadline. August the twelfth." Why was it he always sounded like a kid when he argued with his mother? A whining kid. He cleared his throat, brought his head up so that his eyes met hers. "It's something I've got to do, and I can't do it nights, not after a day's hard work. I may not be able to do it at all, but I've got to try. Don't you see it's just as important right now to learn I'm not a playwright as it is to learn that I am. I've got to get it out of my craw, don't you see?"

"I see," his mother said softly. So softly he was afraid his father might not have heard.

But he did, for in a moment he said, "I'm not an unreasonable man. If it's hard, physical work that will interfere, and don't misunderstand me, I prefer manual labor for a young man not out of college, but if that is the problem, I'm sure we could find something for you to do at the office. The important thing is that you keep constructively occupied."

So here they were, Johnny thought hopelessly, round Robin Hood's barn and back again. Constructively occupied! And just how did an English major go about keeping constructively occupied in an architectural firm? Run errands? Empty wastebaskets? And not only would there be his father lording it over him all day, but there would be Garfield Sumner. Garfield Sumner, his father's partner. That's the way he tried to think of him. Just that and no more. Not Cara's husband. Once in a while he'd see them together. Garfield and Cara. But he never got used to it. And he knew he'd never get used to working in the same office with Garfield Sumner.

"I've got to finish this play," he said. "I've got to finish it before the middle of August. If I finish it before then I'll go to work on any damned job you want me to, but I've got to finish. Even if it means leaving..."

"Please," his mother interrupted, "don't be impulsive."

"Even if it means what?" His father had given up all pretense to patience.

"Even if it means moving out of here," Johnny said.

"Hah!" His father scored, "Then you *would* have to go to work."

"I'd use some of the money Aunt..."

"Please, both of you," his mother pleaded. "Can't we have a cooling-off period? Frank, you're already late for the office, and I have a million things to do ... Johnny..."

"OK, Mom, OK," Johnny said. He knew what she meant by a cooling-off period. She meant time to work on them both. Separately. Sometimes he felt an enormous compassion for her, this slender, clear-eyed woman with her beautiful hands, her grave smile, her mercurial moods, this woman who was their mother. Sometimes he wondered just what she got out of it.

Next door the doctor pronounced Cara Sumner dead presumably of suffocation and called the police and the Chicago hotel where Garfield Sumner had been registered and no longer was, and a sister of Cara's in Oklahoma, and the offices of Sumner and Merrill where he left word to have either Mr. Merrill or Mr. Sumner call him as soon as they arrived.

Marny, who had slipped in the side door just as the police came through the front hall, had trailed them upstairs and into Cara's bedroom before they thought to ask her who she was and what she was doing there. They shooed her out and down the stairs. All she'd seen was Cara's hair flowing across the pillow and the green dress with the turtle doves on it lying crumpled on the floor beside the dressing table. The hair looked alive, but the dress didn't. She went to the kitchen to find someone who could tell her what the matter was, but there was no one in the kitchen, so she went home. She met Johnny storming out of the dining room. Her mother and father were still at the breakfast table arguing about Johnny's character. She stood in the doorway and told them that something had happened to Cara. They looked at her without seeming to see her.

"He's still so young, just a boy really in many ways, and not like you in the least," her mother was saying. "You must try to ..."

"That's the trouble with him. When I was his age I'd worked every summer for ten years and half the winters, too. He's no playwright, and you know it. If he were, he'd get it written one way or another. Nothing could stop him!" Her father's fist pounded the table. "I may not know much about writers, but I know this much. The only ones worth their salt were men to start with."

"Something"—Marny tried again in a slightly higher

key—"has happened to Cara, but I don't know what. Not exactly." She wasn't really frightened. She'd seen enough on television of policemen in ladies' bedrooms not to be frightened. And when the ladies were pretty and kind, it usually turned out all right in the end.

"Darling," her mother said. "Why aren't you in swimming?"

"Because you told me not to go in unless Cara could watch me, and she couldn't." Unexpectedly a tear formed in the corner of her eye, and another and another. She ran to her mother, the tears spilling out and over and running down her face. "I think she's dead," she said.

"Darling, darling," her mother soothed, and she could feel her smile at her father over the top of her head. "You mustn't jump at such appalling conclusions. Too much TV! Cara always sleeps late. You know that. Did you go to her room?" Marny nodded. "And she was asleep?"

"I don't know. I don't know. I didn't get to see her. The policemen sent me away."

Upstairs in his room Johnny picked up page one, Act One, of *The Peacemakers,* read it through, put it down, retrieved a half-smoked package of cigarettes from the windowsill. He emptied an ashtray into the wastebasket and put it beside the cigarettes on his desk and then he went and looked at himself in the mirror. Gray green eyes, sandy hair, a mouth still in the making. "The question is," he said to the mirror, "have you got it? The drive, the perseverance, and the God-given other thing they call talent?" The face that looked back at him wasn't a man's face, but it wasn't a boy's face either. Bless Cara for that, he thought and turned the thought off. He didn't allow himself to think of Cara in the morning in this room or at any time when he should be writing. It was a rule he'd made. One of many. He didn't allow himself to think of Cara nor to smoke more than one cigarette every five hundred words nor to open any book except the dictionary and Roget's Thesaurus.

From the mirror he walked to the window. There was no rule about that. His room was on the side of the house away from the Sumner place. He looked down on his mother's rose garden and the top of the garage. Not that the Sumner house itself held any associations for him. The lake cottage housed all that he wished to be reminded of, but still any place that held Cara would prove distracting even though the Cara who lived next door was a stranger to him. She saw to that. Sometimes it filled him with impotent rage, at others with tears, but for the most part he was grateful to her that this was so.

He went finally to his desk and sat down, rolled a blank piece of paper into the typewriter.

Page Eleven.

(*Exit* ROBERTO. *With his going the two girls relax.* ELIZABETH *slides down onto the sofa, kicking off her shoes.*)

ELIZABETH: You're no good for him, you know. Someday when it's too late, he'll find it out and hate you for it.

MARCIA: But in the meantime . . .

Just as the world started slipping away and he was in that living room in Greenwich Village, really there, knowing what the voices of those girls sounded like, almost but not quite knowing what they must say, he heard a door slam downstairs, heard Marny run past his door stifling a sob. Swearing aloud he jumped up and put a record on the record player and turned the volume up as far as it would go. It was Beethoven. Beethoven could drown out anything. And at the same time leave you alone. Leave you alone with two half-baked girls fighting for the soul of a man in a Greenwich Village apartment. He sighed contentedly and resumed his slow, uneven typing.

Frank Merrill had played football at college and afterward professional football for a year or two before the Army got him. He was large and handsome in a direct and stubborn way. His mind, like his body, moved slowly and with infinite coordination. Listening to Marny's explanation of why she'd not gone swimming, he was more amused than alarmed. Marny could lend drama to the most insignificant of circumstances.

"What policemen chased you home?" he teased. "Peter Gunn or one of Perry Mason's boys?"

"Yes," Lindsey said, "what policemen?" He saw that Lindsey looked anything but amused.

"Just policemen," Marny said, her voice catching. "They wanted to know who I was and what I was doing there. I told them, and they told me, at least one of them told me, to run along home."

"I thought policemen always say 'scram,'" he said, but even as he said it he realized there was something in the child's eyes, a mute tearful pleading that told him this was all wrong this teasing, this joking. He pushed back his chair.

To Lindsey he said, "Perhaps I'd better run over for a minute and check."

"I think perhaps you should," Lindsey said, and as he went out the door he saw her gently remove Marny from her lap, heard her say, "It'll be all right. You'll see. Daddy'll get it all straight."

If he'd gone in the front way he would have seen the doctor's car and the police car, but the side entrance was nearer. It had no bell, so he walked in and through the dining room into the hall. He started toward the back of the house where he hoped to find one of the servants, but the sound of heavy footsteps and men's voices above stairs stopped him. He wheeled and walked to the stairs and up them. A man he'd never seen before was standing in the upper hall talking to the maid who, flushed and tearful, seemed to be having trouble hearing whatever it was he said.

"What's happened here?" he said, beginning to feel the tightening in his abdomen that always assailed him in moments of crisis.

"Oh, Mr. Merrill," the maid turned a distraught face, "I'm so glad you've come." For a moment he was afraid she would throw her arms about him and instinctively braced himself.

"I'm Dr. Farrow," the strange man said, and held out his hand. "I'm not their doctor, but the maid . . ."

"I was so upset their rightful doctor's name went clean out of my head. I just grabbed at the first name . . ."

"Are you a friend of Mrs. Sumner's?" Dr. Farrow said.

"Her husband's partner. We live next door," he said curtly. What did the fellow want? Credentials?

"Then I've bad news for you. Very bad." Dr. Farrow cocked his head and squinted as though he wished to gauge the impact of the blow he was about to deliver. "Mrs. Sumner died last night."

But he'd already guessed at something of the sort. He waited for the rest. It was slow in coming. Dr. Farrow, accustomed to the question and answer method of dealing with these delicate matters, didn't know what to do with Frank's silence.

"I gather Mr. Sumner is on his way home from Chicago," he finally said nervously. "We've not been able to get in touch with him. Perhaps someone would meet his plane. Perhaps you . . ."

"Of course, of course," Frank said, "but what shall I tell him?"

"His plane is due at noon," the maid said. "I got that from his secretary."

"I'll be there," Frank said impatiently. "But what shall

I tell him happened to his wife?" The tightness in his abdomen had become a cramp almost.

"Perhaps you'd better not tell him the whole truth," Dr. Farrow said, "not right off. She was strangled. With a scarf. The police are in there now." He jerked his head to indicate the closed door of Cara's room. "Nasty business," he murmured and backed into a nearby bathroom.

Even when he knew a thing Frank was a man who had to see for himself. It was the same way with the houses he built. Drawings, estimates were necessary, fine, but in the end he always worked from a model. He now walked to the closed door of Cara's room, and without knocking, turned the knob. There was a police officer and what he guessed must be a plainclothes man. Intent, absorbed, detached, they were examining the windowsill. When they heard him they turned, and he saw by the quick change of expression on their faces that they thought he was Garfield . . . Their faces were instantly heavy with sympathy. Comical, if this were any place for comedy. To put an end to it, he told them who he was. They looked not so much relieved as annoyed, and he realized he actually had no business barging in and said so. They didn't argue the point, so he left. But not before he had taken one long look at the bed where Cara lay covered by a sheet with only a few strands of red gold hair splaying out over the pillow to prove that it was she.

Walking back to his own house past the vegetable garden that had been Cara's creation and pride, he thought about how he could break it to Lindsey. Garfield he'd have to think about on the way to the airport. First things first. And with Garfield he could count on the man's dignity, his reserve, but Lindsey . . . He never knew with Lindsey. Never had. Never would. Any total knowledge he'd ever hoped to have of her had evaded him from the moment she'd first surrendered to him. Oh,

Everybody Adored Cara 19

he knew pretty well how she would react to the little things, the day's headlines, the weather, a flat tire, a gift, but the big ones . . . there just never was any telling. Like the time she'd miscarried their first child. He'd thought naturally she'd go to pieces for a while, but she hadn't. Quite the contrary. She'd seemed to acquire a new serenity, a gentleness toward him and everyone. Baffling. Like the time returning late at night from a dance they had witnessed an accident in which a young girl was killed. The girl was a stranger, and they'd not even seen her. They'd been told by someone that she'd died, but Lindsey had wept for days afterward at odd and unlikely moments with an abandon that made him feel awkward and helpless.

He found her in the kitchen washing the breakfast dishes. Hearing his step, she turned, tensely erect. "Well?" she said, her lips stayed parted over the word, and her eyes searching his were wide and questioning. When he didn't answer her at once, she came to him and put her arms around his neck and looked up at him beseechingly.

"There's nothing *really* wrong, is there? There can't be. Cara's healthy as can be and . . . it just can't be anything really . . ."

"I'm afraid it can," he said.

"Then what? Tell me." With her arms she gave his shoulder a little shake.

"Marny was right. Cara's dead."

"But how? She didn't, she wouldn't, she just isn't the kind . . ." Shock, disbelief clouded her eyes. He hadn't until that moment thought of suicide. He didn't think of it long now. Strangled with a scarf, the doctor had said. That was not something you could do to yourself.

"Of course not," he said aloud, and then because Lindsey was still looking at him in that beseeching way, he heard himself saying, "They don't know yet."

"It must have been her heart, something like that that she never even guessed about. Something sudden. Maybe an aneurysm like that Jones woman." Lindsey's arms dropped to her sides, and she let herself down in the chair next to the kitchen table. "I used to envy her her vitality. Was it in her sleep? I hope that's the way it was. Funny, I keep feeling I should go to her. Does Garfield know? Is he back?"

"No. I'm to meet his plane."

"Poor Frank, that won't be easy. Do you want me to come with you?"

"Not unless you want to."

"Heaven forbid! I, I . . . Well, anyway I should stay here and have a talk with Marny. It must have been an awful shock for her. Do you suppose she saw . . . Frank! What was it she said about policemen?" With the memory, her hand flew to her throat. "Did she make it up?"

"No," he said wretchedly. He might have known he couldn't fool her for long.

"Then?"

"It looks as though someone did her in."

"Killed her?"

"Strangled her. With a scarf."

"Oh my God, Frank. You can't mean that. Murder? Cara?"

"That's the way it looks."

"But everyone adored her," Lindsey said, and began to cry silent tears against the back of her hand. He never knew what to do when she cried. Never knew what she wanted him to do. Sometimes she wanted comfort. Sometimes she wanted to be left alone.

"It was probably a prowler . . . someone looking for money or jewelry," he said, but as he said it he was remembering Cara's room and how orderly, except for a garment of clothing or two on the floor, everything had been. Perhaps the police . . . but they wouldn't, they'd leave everything just as they found it, wouldn't they? Wasn't that a rule?

"How ghastly. This sort of thing just doesn't happen,

Everybody Adored Cara 21

Frank. Not to nice people. Not in quiet neighborhoods." She dabbed at her eyes with the back of her hand. "Monstrous!" she whispered and got up and went to the sink and scooped water on her face.

"Try not to think about it," he said.

"You do think of the most remarkable solutions," she laughed shortly, but then she kissed him to make up for it. "Isn't it about time you were going to meet Garfield?"

"Will you be all right?" He still didn't know really what she was feeling. How much. Maybe like him she was still numb.

"I'll just have to be." She gave him a wavering smile.

The road to the airport was shaded and wound through farmlands and around pastures. It reminded him of a road he'd used to take as a boy out in Ohio when he wanted to be alone. Wanted to get away from his mother's drinking and his father's rages and the hurt, accusing eyes of his younger brothers and sisters looking to him for the answer because he was the oldest.

He thought about what to say to Garfield. Why was it that at times like this the clichés were all that came to mind. "I'm afraid I've got some pretty rotten news for you!" Not strong enough. Garfield would think they'd missed out on the library contract, something like that. Hell, he couldn't think of more than two or three times in their almost twenty years of association when they'd discussed anything more intimate than business.

There'd been the time when Garfield had told him that he and Helen, his first wife, were going to get a divorce. "I, we are wretched," he'd said. "We do nothing for each other." It had taken Frank's shocked disbelief to draw him out further. "We never should have married. It was something we drifted into after long acquaintance. But there's no spark, there never has been."

Frank could buy that much. Helen Sumner was not a woman to ignite sparks, but neither was she one to feel acutely the lack. She had always seemed to him and to Lindsey, though they didn't pretend to understand her, serenely content with her lot. And though one never really knew what Garfield was feeling, he had always treated her with such kindness and courtesy that one assumed. . . . "How does Helen feel about this divorce?" Frank had blurted and, at that, Garfield had flushed.

"I might as well tell you that she's resisted the idea. The accoutrements of marriage, home, friends, position, it would seem mean much more to a woman." He had looked both defensive and angry. "It hasn't been easy," he finished on a note intended to close the subject.

Far more revealing had been the time much later, months after he and Cara were married, when they were having a picnic supper at the lake cottage, just the four of them. They had spent the afternoon fishing, had eaten sumptuously and now Frank and Garfield lolled at opposite ends of the big leather sofa while Cara and Lindsey sat cross-legged in front of the fire toasting marshmallows and talking to each other in low voices designed not so much to shut them out as to spare them the frivolity of their woman-talk. Cara, her smile lighted by some remark of Lindsey's turned to offer her husband a marshmallow. The firelight enhanced her hair and flickered softly across her face and when she'd turned away again, Garfield said, very softly so that she should not hear, "Isn't she marvelous? Whatever do you suppose she sees in me?" There had been honest wonder in the query and Frank should have liked to give him an answer but it was not the sort of answer that could be given easily and in the presence of the woman of whom he spoke. However, it was obvious to almost everyone who knew them that those very things in himself which Garfield found most difficult to reconcile with Cara's youth, his conservatism, his caution, even his rigidity, were the very things that had attracted and held her. Without him, she would undoubtedly become rudderless and lost and she knew it. It was too bad Garfield couldn't know it, too. Or couldn't believe it.

But this reminiscing was getting him nowhere, and he would be at the airport in a few minutes. He tried putting himself in Garfield's place. If he were Garfield ... But he wasn't, and he was no good at putting himself in someone else's shoes. He could sometimes guess what people were thinking, never what they were feeling. Or not feeling.

He was late. The plane had landed. Garfield was hurrying toward him across the airstrip, a tall, lean man, impeccably dressed. He didn't appear at all surprised to see Frank, and in an unprecedented gesture of warmth took his hand in both of his.

"Good of you to come." It wasn't only the handclasp that told him that Garfield already knew. It was the dark glasses. Garfield never wore them. He considered them bad form. "Dark glasses," he'd heard him say more than once, "are for the beach or people with bad eyes. Or beggars!" Today Garfield must have learned that they are also for privacy.

"I wanted to come," Frank said and abruptly Garfield let go his hand, and they were striding across the airstrip toward Frank's car as though it were another plane to be caught. "I didn't know you'd heard," Frank said.

"The office had me paged at Idlewild," Garfield replied briefly. They reached the car, and for a moment Garfield's hand on the door faltered. "Cara always met my plane," he said, and opened the door and climbed in, his long legs mocking the compact little German car.

As Frank maneuvered them out of the parking lot and onto the highway, Garfield removed his dark glasses, wiped them slowly, thoughtfully, with a clean handkerchief and put them back on. "I talked to her last night," he said huskily and cleared his throat. "Just last night. I can't take it in. I can't take it in at all ..."

"Don't try to," Frank said and wondered just how

much the office had told him. If he'd talked to Miss Timmons, she'd have protected him, but if it had been Rose Caldwell, he probably knew everything there was to know, even down to the color of the chiffon scarf around Cara's neck.

"It's got to be a thief or a madman who'd do a thing like that," Garfield answered his unspoken question. "Everyone liked Cara. Even the servants. She has a way with people. She's . . . I mean she was . . . God damn it, Frank!" He leaned forward and brought his fists down on his knees. "I don't believe it. It's crazy, crazy . . ." He broke off and bent his head against his clenched fists.

Cathy and Bibsy sat at a table in The Purple Window studying the menu, or trying to. They were much too excited to put their minds seriously on anything.

"Stone's yet! Wait'll I tell Johnny." Cathy, elbows on the table, clasped her hands beneath her chin. "He was so scornful this morning. I think he honestly believed we'd end up running the popcorn machine at the dime store."

"Did he know we were going together, that I was going to be with you?"

"I think I told him."

"What did he say?" Bibsy peered over the top of the menu at her friend, and in her eyes there was an unconscious look of pleading.

"I told you . . . that we'd end up running . . ."

"I don't mean *that*. I mean about me, did he say anything about me? I used to think"—she blushed and let the menu drop—"well, frankly, I used to think he liked me a lot. Used to, that is. Lately I don't know what to think."

"Nobody does," Cathy sighed. "He's writing a play."

"How marvelous! What about?"

"I don't know. He says if he talks about it, he won't want to write it."

"I wish you'd do me a favor."

"You know if I can I will."

"Tell him I asked about him." Bibsy flushed and, looking about to make sure none of her mother's friends were present, she drew out a package of cigarettes. Her mother thought smoking was "cheap," smoking and eye shadow and the way everyone was wearing their hair now, everyone but Bibsy. "Only the rich," her mother was always saying, "can afford to be cheap." "I think," Bibsy said, "I'll order the *filet de sole*." She had no idea it was just plain fish, and was appalled when it was set before her. She loathed fish. But with Cathy there, Cathy who could afford to wear eye shadow and hair like a rat's nest, Cathy who, in this the town's most fancy lunch spot, had confidently ordered a hamburger, she felt compelled to eat it.

After lunch they decided to stay downtown and see a movie. But Cathy, unable to contain her triumph a moment longer, called her mother. Her mother didn't seem the slightest interested or impressed. Her "How very nice, dear" was both preoccupied and slow in coming. Didn't her mother realize this was one of the big moments in her life? She wished she'd called Cara instead and would have had she had another dime.

After Frank left for the airport, Lindsey went upstairs and knocked on the closed door of Marny's room. She had no idea what she would say to the child. Her own thoughts and feelings were in such confusion. But it was something to be doing, and she did want to say something before whatever Marny had seen next door had hardened into ugly truth. Though what was there to say when you came right down to it? This was no television fright that could be banished with a Popsicle, a hug, and a don't be silly, darling, it's all just make-believe. Maybe you didn't say anything, maybe you just...

"Come in," Marny said.

Her room was small with sloping ceilings and bright yellow walls. She was sitting cross-legged on her bed, a book propped open on her knees. The book was *The Tailor of Gloucester,* a story about an elderly, ailing tailor and some kindly mice. Over a year ago Marny had declared it much too babyish.

Marny never threw away or gave away anything. Tables, chairs, the window seat held the surviving remnants of her eight years. Push toys, rag dolls, Teddy bears, plastic dolls, paste, paints, a collection of empty perfume bottles and another of butterflies mounted on a plyboard screen fought for space. Lindsey picked her way around a pair of shoes, riding boots, and a mammoth block house to the one available chair. Marny scowled up at her through fronds of brown hair that had got loose from her barrette. "Now do you believe me?" she said crossly.

"Believe you?"

"About Cara being dead?"

"Yes, dear, I'm afraid we do."

"Daddy laughed at me," she said, her voice catching.

"But darling, he didn't mean anything by it. You must know it was a hard thing to . . . well, naturally we didn't want to believe it." She broke off dismayed at the turn the conversation had taken.

"He laughed at me and teased me and thought I told a lie."

"It was nothing personal, you silly goose. If it had been Cathy who'd told us we wouldn't have believed her right away either." Lindsey, listening to her own voice going on in this matter of fact way, thought, the thing is I still don't really believe it. I wonder if Marny does . . . I wonder how much she saw . . . seeing is believing . . . but not always.

"Did someone kill her?" Marny closed the book and put it down beside her on the bed. Lindsey's instinct was to deny this, but when she tried to voice her protest, no sound came. What was the use? There would be the newspapers, the comings and goings next door, the talk.

"What makes you ask that?" she stalled.

"Because of the policemen. Because she wasn't sick yesterday. And she wasn't sick last night."

"Last night?"

"She went out last night," Marny pointed to the west window which looked down on the Sumners' backyard. "I couldn't go to sleep, so I stayed up and looked for satellites, and I saw her go out. I didn't find a satellite. You can tell, you know. They move slower than planes."

"I suppose they do," Lindsey said absently. "Was anyone with Cara when she went out?"

"I didn't see anybody, but I still think somebody killed her," Marny said, the catch coming back into her voice.

"We don't know that," Lindsey said. "Besides, it's not important how she died. The important thing is how she lived and to remember her that way, how happy she was, and gay, and how much she gave everyone." But Lindsey could see Marny wasn't listening, and she didn't blame her.

"Who do *you* think killed her?" Marny said.

"Darling, darling," Lindsey cried despairingly, "you mustn't talk that way. You mustn't even think that way. Look, how would you like to take a picnic lunch out to the lake, just the two of us. I could take my paints, and you could have a swim, and we . . ."

"I'd much rather stay here," Marny said. "I've got a awful stomach-ache," she said and began very softly to cry. Lindsey went and scooped her up in her arms and retrieving *The Tailor of Gloucester,* returned to the chair. "In the town of Gloucester there lived a tailor . . ."

The text did not fully engage her, her unclaimed thoughts flew off in all directions . . . she must see to the back door lock, a new one was probably in order. The old one hadn't really worked in months. It might just as well have been their house entered, violated . . . what a horrible way to die. At the hands of a stranger. But supposing it had not been a stranger? Unthinkable. How I shall miss her! Not that we were ever terribly intimate, the way some women are, sharing everything, including their husband's secrets. Heaven forbid! Good friends. Good neighbors. I shall miss her gaiety, her joy in little things. A book, an unexpected letter, a new recipe, and her day was made. Poor Garfield. If ever a man was captivated . . . I don't think he had the slightest notion about love until Cara came along. How dismal that first marriage must have been. He and Helen as alike as peas in a pod. Austere, proper, proud. No wonder they found nothing to talk about. Funny how long ago and far away that seems. Unreal. Oh Cara, what happened? Did it take long? Were you afraid?

"The book is shaking," Marny said, "and I can't see the pictures."

At about one o'clock Johnny began to feel hungry. He lighted a cigarette and reread his morning's work. The scene between the two girls was going along fine, but he'd have to watch this tendency to make Elizabeth like Cara. She wasn't like her at all. It would throw everything out of kilter if he made her so. He supposed all artists had trouble keeping their women out of their work. Making a mental note to change Elizabeth's eyes to brown and her hair to black, he went downstairs in search of food.

There was no formal lunch hour. His father ate downtown usually, and whoever was at home plundered the icebox. He hoped his mother and Marny had eaten. He was in no mood for small talk. However, the kitchen was empty, and now that he thought about it, the house was awfully quiet and had been all morning except for Marny snuffling past his door hours earlier. He wondered what that had been all about. Usually when Marny cried

Everybody Adored Cara

she gave it the works. Maybe the kid was growing up.

In the icebox he found cheese, a half-used can of deviled ham, and a few tomatoes. He put them on a plate with some bread and a jar of mayonnaise and carried them to the table underneath the kitchen window. The kitchen windows faced the southeast portion of the Sumner house and yard. Several cars were parked toward the back of the house near the garage, and Johnny guessed that Cara must be having a luncheon. He couldn't imagine her in the role of hostess to a lot of empty-headed, gabbing females such as attended his mother's various gatherings. There was much that he couldn't imagine about Cara. Doors between them that must be kept closed. This she had insisted on from the start.

He heard the front screen door slam and in a moment his father calling, as he always did the minute he entered the house, for his mother. Johnny started out in the hall to tell his father that she wasn't home, but halfway to the door he heard his mother answer from somewhere upstairs, and he went back to the table and wolfed down the rest of his sandwich.

And then he went out of the kitchen and saw his mother and father in the hall, the two of them together, talking in low, urgent voices. His mother was pale, his father strained. He thought they were quarreling, and when they looked at him he thought they were still quarreling about him. He said, "Look, I hope you two aren't still at it. If I'm going to hell, why don't you just let me go my own way. One summer of digging ditches isn't going to save me. Can't you just . . ."

"How can you think only of yourself at a time like this?" his father said. He didn't sound angry. He sounded tired. Beat. And all of a sudden he felt scared. Not for himself. For them. Something must have happened to them. Business?

"A time like what?" Johnny said. He didn't know,

couldn't remember, which one of them told him. Which one of them said it. But one of them said that Cara was dead. "Didn't you know?" one of them said. He didn't know. He shook his head. So they told him again, only this time they told him more. He had to stay there and listen. Stand there poker-faced and hear them out. And when they'd finished, he had to say something. And he did. He said something, and then he had to walk past them and up the stairs just like it was Mrs. Sumner, their neighbor, they were talking about. And not Cara. He felt their eyes following him. Felt their puzzlement. They think I'm a cold son-of-a-bitch, he thought, and for a moment felt nothing but pride at the way he'd carried it off. But only for a moment. When he finally made his room and shut the door, he went and sat on the edge of his bed to give his legs a rest, because they felt as though they might be going to buckle under him. After he'd been sitting there awhile, he did a thing he'd not done since he was a child. He pinched the skin of his forearm between his thumb and forefinger as hard as he could. But nothing happened. Only a small, sharp pain and himself still sitting there alone on the edge of his bed. So he wasn't dreaming. But that still didn't make it true. It didn't make Cara dead. Just because he wasn't dreaming. They must have lied to him. Made it up to scare him with because they'd heard something. Guessed something. And wanted to trap him into . . . it had to be something like that. A trap. Some damned parent scheme . . . and to hell with him, what it did to him! Abruptly, angrily, he stood up. Anger put the strength back into his legs, but his throat and mouth felt parched, aching. He went into the bathroom and sloshed down three glasses of water, and then he started down the stairs to face them. To confront them with his fury. His contempt. To have it out for once and all. But they weren't there. Not in the living room nor the television room, nor on the porch. In the kitchen he encountered Marny perched on a stool eating a dish of ice cream. She was wearing pajamas, and her hair flopped around her face like the hair of a Sealyham terrier.

"I'm sick," she said importantly.

"Where's Father?" he said, hoarding his anger, not wanting it deflected.

"Over at the Sumners'. Mother, too."

The anger, the disbelief that had served as narcotic were beginning to wear off. "What are they doing over there?"

"Helping with everything."

"Everything?" he said, and wished the question back. He knew now. He knew, and he didn't need any little eight-year-old girl telling it to him all over again.

" 'Rangements and . . ."

"Never mind," he said harshly and turned swiftly to hide whatever might be showing in his eyes. "Never mind," he repeated on a note of anguish and made for the back door.

"Don't leave me," Marny cried out. "I'll be all alone if you do. They said you'd be here. Please." Her voice followed him out and down the driveway. "I'm scared, Johnny, please . . ." He even imagined he heard it above the roaring of the jalopy's motor as he sped across town and out Hingham Road, "Don't leave me!" But presently it was his own voice, crying, sobbing as he drove: "Don't leave me!"

The sight of the cottage at the lake's edge quieted him. Here was reality. Here was Cara. He drove past the house and parked the jalopy, as had always been their habit, on the little-used road leading to the old boathouse. He got out of the jalopy and walked toward the cottage. It was more than a cottage actually, two big stone chimneys, and two big porches, lakeside and woods-side, but that is what his father had always called it, and he should know. He'd designed it. For his mother. Ten years ago. It was hard any more to think of the place as existing for anyone except Cara. And himself.

The two of them. But today as he walked toward it, it seemed to drift and waver before his eyes, and when he tried to put the key in the lock of the front door, he found his hand was shaking so that he couldn't. With an oath he let the key drop and went down to the dock and ripped off his clothes and dived naked into the chill, pale blue water. He swam out to the float and back, and when he hoisted himself back up on the dock, he was shivering, but his head was clear. He was thinking again. And what he was thinking was that if it was all true and Cara was dead and someone had killed her, it was probably Garfield. Maybe he'd found the locket, maybe he'd found out about him giving her a lift to the supermarket the day before she died. She'd wanted to see him, to tell him something which she'd never got around to telling him. . . . That was it. Garfield! Sneaking back from Chicago. Maybe it hadn't had anything to do with him, Johnny, at all. Maybe it had to do with the way Cara froze whenever he tried to talk about her marriage. Maybe it had to do with the thing he never understood about that marriage—why she'd married anyone as old and stuffy as Garfield in the first place. Whatever it had to do with it, it had to be Garfield. It had to be because that was the only thing that made any sense at all.

He was still shivering when he climbed into his clothes and went up to the cottage to try the key again. Inside the cottage was just as he'd left it the evening before. The charred logs from the fire he'd lit against the sunset cool of the June evening exuded an autumn smell, and the pillow on the couch where he had lain dreaming impossible dreams of Cara, still held the hollow of his head. He hurled himself down on the couch, and burying his face in the haunted pillow, wept.

It was twilight when Cathy and Bibsy emerged teary-eyed and trancelike from the movie theater.

"I think I'd have liked it better if Rachel hadn't had to die," Bibsy said wistfully. "And yet I suppose it was that last scene that made the picture, lifted it out of the ordinary, I mean."

"Oh, she had to die," Cathy said. "I think you almost knew that from the beginning. Otherwise you couldn't have stood it, not possibly."

"The one I felt really sorry for," Bibsy said, "was the little girl."

At the corner of Main and Bradley a newsboy waved an afternoon paper under their noses. Bibsy shook her head, but Cathy, reaching in her bag, gave him a quarter.

"Goodness," Bibsy said, "this job *has* gone to your head."

"I'm sure it has," Cathy said, "but he did look hungry."

"All little boys look hungry."

At the bus stop Cathy unfolded the paper. "Ah, good, fair tomorrow. Don't you think we should get up a gang and have one last fling at the lake before . . ."

Looking over her shoulder Bibsy said: "Prominent socialite found murdered. Really! With the whole world teetering on the verge of war, this makes the front page. Just because she's social register! I could get killed tomorrow and not get beyond the obituaries."

"Oh, I don't know," Cathy said. "Murder is always big news. Besides, I've noticed they call anyone with a two-car garage in a semirespectable neighborhood a prominent socialite. If they get murdered, that is."

"That still doesn't include me in," Bibsy said.

Their bus came to a gaseous stop, and they climbed aboard. They couldn't get seats together. Cathy found herself next to a woman whose dimensions were such that only by sitting with her legs in the aisle could she share the seat at all. Any further reading of the paper was impossible. And though her curiosity had been aroused by the headline it was too dark when they got off the bus to decipher the fine print. She and Bibsy parted at the corner near Bibsy's house, and Cathy, seeing how fast the twilight was fading, hurried toward home. By the time she reached Fair Avenue the street lights were on and, waiting for a break in the traffic so she might cross, she reread the provocative headline, and holding the paper up to the light, read the first few lines beneath it: *Mrs. Garfield Sumner, wife of a prominent architect here, was found dead this morning at her home in suburban Wingate* . . . She pushed the paper under her arm and crossed the avenue. If it were true, why hadn't her mother told her when she called? She wished Bibsy were still along. She wished it weren't so dark. Before she could reach her house, she must pass Cara's house. She didn't know what she expected, but nothing seemed changed at all. There were a few lights on inside but not many. The windows of Cara's room were dark, but then they often were at this time of the evening. She didn't pause or even slow her pace, and when she saw the lights of her own house, she began to run toward them.

She found her parents in the living room having their usual before-dinner highball. She didn't know how she'd expected to find them, but somehow this shocked her.

"Is it true about Cara?" she said, her voice heavy with accusation. "I simply couldn't believe it." She waved the paper at them. "Why didn't you tell me? Why didn't you tell me when I called?"

"I debated . . ." her mother said, "but I didn't want to spoil your afternoon."

Cathy saw now that her mother looked exhausted, ill almost, but her own emotions left no room for compassion. "How could you let me go on as though nothing had happened. How could you be so unfeeling?"

"Catherine!" her father said. She'd not heard him say it in just that way since she was about twelve. "Your mother, all of us, have been through quite enough today. And this is only the beginning."

"I'm sorry," she mumbled, "but it was awful just reading it like that on a street corner . . ."

"I'd no idea the papers would have the story so soon," her mother said.

"What do they say?" her father said.

"They said she was murdered . . ." It was half-statement, half-question, though of course she knew. She handed her father the sheets which she still held under her arm. "Do they know who did it? It must have been somebody out of their mind. Was it one of these . . . ?" She'd been about to say rapists, but found it was a word she was reluctant to use in terms of Cara, and let the sentence hang.

"We don't know anything yet, dear."

"The sooner they know and catch him, the happier I'll be," Cathy said and shivered.

"Is that all that concerns you?"

"Of course not," she said, "but it is something to think about. Especially when I can't think about Cara, about her being dead . . ."

"Forgive me," her mother said. "We're all strung up. Why don't you go upstairs and get a bath before supper. You'd be surprised how soothing a bath can be."

Supper! How could they think about food! And yet now that they'd made her think about it, she found to her astonishment that she was hungry. "I suppose," she said aloud, "that it's important to keep things going along as usual."

"We must try," her mother said, and for one incredible moment she thought she saw a look of near panic in her mother's eyes, but it was so fleeting, so out of character, that it was easy to decide she'd imagined it. "We've sent Marny to the Browns' for a day or two," her mother continued. "Johnny went off and left her alone in the house. She was in such a state when we got back that I thought it best to get her away, among children her own age."

"Where is Johnny?" It seemed years ago that she'd been looking forward to telling him about her job.

"We don't know."

"Fiddling while Rome burns!" her father said and gave the newspaper an ominous shake. "By the way, congratulations on your job." Her father tried valiantly for a note of enthusiasm. "Oh, it's nothing," Cathy said, and the worst of it was that it had begun to feel like nothing. Nothing at all. There was not one ounce of joy or triumph left in her.

Midway up the stairs she paused, half-tempted to tell them that she didn't want a bath, that she was afraid to be alone up there, but just then Johnny came in, and she didn't want him to know what a baby she was.

The moment Lindsey saw the boy, she knew this was no time to scold him. He looked drawn and tight lipped, and she was sure that however he'd passed the last few hours they'd not been easy for him. What did Frank expect him to do? He couldn't stay glued to his desk with tragedy squatting next door. He might not be as personally involved as the rest of them, but he was sensitive and emotional and incapable of the sort of detachment Frank credited him with. She wished to God she could head Frank off and knew with a hopelessness close to tears that she couldn't.

"Where have you been?" Frank said.

"Downtown. Here and there. Got the brakes fixed on my car . . ."

"We depended on you to be here. With Marny."

"You didn't tell me . . ."

"She did. She says she pleaded with you. The child was upset. You could see that. How could you walk out on her? Don't you realize what's happened today? Cara's death is only the half of it. Marny's world is shaken. Ours too. For God's sake, aren't you man enough to see, to feel for somebody besides yourself? To stick around and offer a hand? Maybe Cara meant nothing to you, but she meant something to the rest of us. And the way she died should have meant something to you. Murder next door, and you go off and get the brakes on your car fixed!" All the day's withheld shock, bafflement, and pain exploded in his voice. He half-rose from his chair. Johnny had turned so pale that Lindsey was afraid he was going to be sick. Right there on the carpet. It was what used to happen when he was little. And afraid.

"Please, Frank!" she cried, but so absorbed was their anger that she doubted if either heard.

"You hate me, don't you?" Johnny's voice was, Lindsey thought, remarkably controlled, and though it was to his father that he spoke, it was her heart that leaped in despair, her eyes that flooded.

"My own son! Don't be a fool!"

"Then lay off," Johnny said. "Get off my back." He turned and started from the room, but Lindsey rose and ran after him.

"Darling, you mustn't . . . we mustn't. This is no time . . ."

"Dinner is ready, Mrs. Merrill," Tina, the three-nights-a-week cook, said from the hall.

"Dinner?" Johnny said. "You mean to say you're going to sit down and eat tonight? Eat food?" He threw back his head and laughed, but there was no merriment in the sound. Only derision.

"Of course," Lindsey said firmly. "Will you go upstairs and get Cathy?"

"Sure, Mom, sure." Suddenly all the fight seemed to go out of him. "I'm sorry about Marny," he said. "I wasn't thinking."

"None of us are," she said, and following him out into the hall said, "Please be patient with your father. This is a terrible thing that has happened. I don't think you realize yet quite how terrible . . ." But Johnny was looking at her so strangely that she stopped.

"Poor Mother," he said, and suddenly leaned and kissed the top of her head and, turning abruptly, lumbered up the stairs.

Next door Garfield Sumner sat in the kitchen drinking coffee with Link Jones, chief of the Stoningham police. It was a session that had started hours ago upstairs in Cara's room, had moved from there to the study, and was now winding up, he hoped, here.

He and Link had had adjoining desks two years running in the Stoningham grammar school, and one summer had built a lean-to in Harbens Woods which they'd planned to use for camping during the deer season, but when fall came, Garfield had been sent off to preparatory school, and that had been pretty much the end of that. He tried now, looking at the big, balding man sitting across the table from him, to equate him with the boy. But it was hard to do. The boy had been small and lithe and merry. The boy had wanted to be a doctor.

"So you're positive," Link was saying, "nothing's missing but the locket?"

"I'm not positive of anything, but so far the locket's the only thing."

"And you've no idea what it's worth?"

"No. I told you I didn't give it to her. It didn't look as though it were worth much as jewels go, but she always kept it in the same box with her pearls. That's how I missed it." He shrugged and got up and refilled his cup.

"Left the pearls and took the locket," Link mused. "May not seem like much to you, but it's the first lead we've got . . ."

"It seems like a lot to me. That's why I told you." Garfield rubbed thumb and forefinger to his aching forehead. He sighed. He'd never been so tired in his life. The beach at Iwo didn't hold a candle to this. To his dismay Link poured himself another cup of coffee, lighted another cigar. He probably, thought Garfield, doesn't think a man *can* sleep at a time like this. He wouldn't have thought so himself two days ago.

"If you don't mind," Link said, reaching into the pocket of his coat from which he withdrew a small soiled blue notebook, "I'd like to read my notes back to you. You might think of something, some little thing . . ."

Resigned, Garfield leaned back, closed his eyes. There was nothing, he knew, in that dirty little notebook that he didn't already know by heart. Link's voice, halting and metallic, was all that kept him awake . . . "No signs of struggle, an almost full bottle of sleeping pills beside the bed from which three or four of the pills might be missing, no abrasions or bruises except for the neck burn made by the scarf and a small bruise at the base of her throat. Last seen by the maid Molly Paget when she left at seven P.M. Her husband talked to her from Chicago at approximately nine o'clock. She sounded tired, said she intended to get to bed early. Rough estimate time of death sometime between eleven and five A.M. No indication of theft . . ."

"The locket," Garfield inserted.

"That comes under clues," Link said. "Anybody'd take a locket and leave pearls isn't any thief. An eccentric maybe, but no thief. No, Gar . . . Mr. Sumner, we still don't have a motive . . . not even close. Main thing is whoever done it isn't any stranger to this house . . . or"—and his voice dropped as though he didn't want to make it too blunt—"to your wife."

"Look," Garfield said, "can't some of this wait? I've had about as much . . ."

"Guess I've been pushing too hard," Link grinned sheepishly, folding the notebook shut, "but when I heard it was your wife I asked to be assigned . . . Figured someone like me with a personal interest, you might say, could do some good."

"Personal interest?" Garfield said.

"Kind of . . . I mean, we had some mighty good times as kids. I'll never forget that shanty we built out in Harbens Woods." He broke off and slapped his knee with his hand, smiling to himself. And Garfield thought, he really means it, "a personal interest"; I've got to learn to trust people. But wasn't that what he'd been telling himself for the past year? And where had it got him? And Cara? Maybe if he hadn't kept telling himself just that . . .

He went into the guest room and without taking off his clothes or pulling back the spread, lay down on one of the stiff guest room beds and slept.

At supper at the Merrills', Lindsey was proud of the effort they made—Cathy, Frank. Even Johnny. They talked, at first nervously, about the coming governor's election, about Berlin, about compulsory education, but gradually they forgot what it was that had driven them to these subjects, and the discussions became warm and vigorous, and, to Lindsey, revealing. How was it she'd never known that Frank didn't believe in compulsory schooling, or that Cathy had real, honest-to-goodness nightmares about war over Berlin, or that Johnny didn't believe in free elections because people tended to take the holy privilege for granted. "The right to vote should be earned," he said, his eyes bright with fervor, and Frank was looking at him for the first time in months, years perhaps, with pride. She hadn't realized how terribly shallow their table talk had been. An exchange of trivialities for the most part, enlivened now and then by a scene. We should do this more often she thought. But with supper over and Tina no longer a witness to the performance, they were at loose ends again. Frank, who proclaimed television the worst thing that had happened to family life since the invention of the automobile, and never watched anything but the news and once in a while a football game, went into the television room and turned the set on to some raucous silliness about a horse, a girl and an orchestra. Cathy joined him there. Johnny, muttering about a snag in his play that needed thinking about, went out into the night. Lindsey stood for a moment uncertainly in the door of the television room, but she knew that for her there would be no solace in that giddily flickering screen, and for the first time since Frank had come walking across the kitchen toward her that morning, she could no longer put off thinking about Cara. First there had been Marny to think about. Then Frank. Now there was only Cara. Throwing a sweater about her shoulders, she went out into the rose garden and sat on the stone steps leading to the fountain that had been Frank's present to her on their last anniversary. Even Cara, who had little use for formal gardens of any kind, had conceded the fountain had a certain charm. "It's Frank's giving it to you," she'd said, "that lends it something . . . it must be a very special sort of love that runs to fountains . . ."

It was only by these rare and somewhat wistful comments on the Merrills' marriage that Cara ever gave any indication that there might be arid areas in her own. These comments were always made in the offhand, casual way Cara had of saying the meaningful things and Lindsey, caught off guard, never knew quite what to say. She guessed what it was Cara missed in her marriage and knew it wasn't at all what Garfield thought she missed. Garfield adored her but he didn't in the least understand her and what she missed was undoubtedly the easy give and take between two people who, though they may not take each other for granted, take their love for granted. Garfield had never seemed to get over the wonder of possessing her, a state of heart which Lindsey imagined could at times prove burdensome to both of them.

She had first seen Cara not in the flesh but in her mind's eye through Garfield's description of her which, like Garfield himself, had been reserved. She was, he'd said, a fashion designer whom he'd met when he lectured at the School of Creative and Applied Design in New York. She was, he'd said small and fair and walked with a slight limp sustained from a riding accident when she was young . . . "Not," he said flushing, "that she's very old now, early thirties, but that should make no difference. I do hope you and she, Lindsey, will be friends. Stoningham is a far cry from New York, and I'm not at all sure . . . well, just to give you an idea, the only times she's ever left New York were to go to London and Paris . . . she hasn't the remotest idea what to expect of life here . . ."

Having left out all the salient details, her warmth, her gaiety, the arresting beauty of her hair, the exquisite proportions of her small-boned body, Lindsey had visualized one of these brash young things with experienced eyes seen on the covers of travel folders, and had wondered how Garfield, with all his caution, could have leaped so quickly, as it were, from the fire into the frying pan. Nor was she reassured by Frank's wry comment that in view of the time that had elapsed since Garfield last lectured at the School of Creative Arts, he must know very well what he was doing. It took only a little calculating to realize that Garfield had known the woman long before he and Helen were divorced. Of course, there was always the possibility that he had simply met her then, and later when he was free looked her up again, but that was most unlikely, and while she'd never been particularly fond of Helen, had always thought the marriage a stultifying arrangement for both of them, she found this explanation of the divorce somehow distasteful and was suddenly cross with Garfield for soliciting her aid in this new venture. Helen as a rigid and cold beauty was one thing. Helen the wronged woman was quite another.

"We don't really ever know anything about anyone," she sighed to Frank.

Yet when she met Cara all her crossness with Garfield vanished. He brought her around one Sunday afternoon a few days after they returned from a brief honeymoon in Canada.

"This is Cara," Garfield said, giving the name such reverence that Lindsey had had to repress a smile. He stood framed in the doorway, his arm encircling the slight fur-clad shoulders of his bride, and beamed upon them with boyish pride, as much a stranger to them in that moment as the woman beside him.

Of course, what she first noticed about Cara was her hair, that was what everyone first saw, and it was misleading. Beneath that silken, aureous crown, one expected a more flourishing beauty. The grave, gray eyes, the pert nose, the tenuously sensuous mouth lacked the prettiness of a more ordered symmetry, and after the impact of the hair you were apt to feel let down.

Lindsey tried to remember what they'd talked about that long-ago Sunday, as though that detached and now utterly meaningless memory might have some bearing . . . but all she could dredge up out of the whole afternoon's hazy passage was herself telling Cara where to shop for meat . . . and she realized that all she'd been doing for the past half hour was playing games, and that nothing had any bearing on Cara's death, because her death was completely out of context. It had to be. And if there was any comfort anywhere, that was it.

Helen Stoney Sumner, Garfield Sumner's first wife, was another who learned of Cara's death from the *Stoningham Evening Press and Standard*. The little town of Hastings, where she'd bought a house after the divorce, was only about seventy-five miles from Stoningham, and much as she'd come to dislike the city where she'd spent her entire married life, she returned on occasion to see her dentist and to attend to real estate holdings which had been a part of her settlement. She made these visits as brief as possible, and shunning those she'd once thought of as her friends, she always stayed at the Stoningham Inn.

The news of her ex-husband's wife leaped out at her from the newsstand just outside the entrance to the inn. She had just completed two wretched hours in and out of the dentist's chair. The Novocaine had begun to wear off, and her jaw throbbed unmercifully. She deposited a coin and gingerly plucked a paper from the dwindling stack. Leaning against the doorway for support, she read or tried to read the story beneath the headlines. But her hands wouldn't hold the paper steady and her vision blurred, jumping words and sentences one on top of the other. She straightened and, folding the paper under her arm, went inside. To the desk clerk she said, "Any messages?" because that was what she always said.

"No messages," he replied without taking his eyes from the paper he was reading. The Mrs. Garfield Sumner whose murder so utterly absorbed him clearly bore no relationship to the woman who stood before him. It astonished Helen that even at this moment that should hurt her.

"Are you sure?" she said harshly, determined to make him at least look at her.

"I am sure." He looked at her then, but dazedly through his preoccupation.

Her room was a corner one facing the afternoon sun. Without waiting to take off hat or gloves she called down an order for ice. Even so, it would be ten minutes or so, and much as she loathed the taste of warm whiskey, she couldn't wait, she was trembling from head to foot. The effects of the Novocaine and on top of that, the shock . . . she tilted a silver flask into the glass in the bathroom and held the glass for a moment under the basin faucet. Still wearing hat and gloves, she took glass and newspaper to the window and holding the paper so that the late afternoon sun hit squarely, illuminating every word, and there could be no mistaking one word for another, she read without joy or sorrow of the death of the woman whom she believed had ruined her life.

Johnny had no idea where he planned to go. It had boiled down simply to all the places he didn't want to be. His room for one. The house for another. But now that he was outside on the dark suburban street with its scattered units of light spelling out the comfort of others, he felt suddenly afraid. This was no animal fear pouring strength, giving adrenaline into the blood, but a cold and empty fear, an old man's fear. Of loneliness. Of weakness. Of final despair. Nowhere to go and no one to talk to, forever and ever and ever.

The sight of the chief of police's car parked at the curb in front of the Sumner house cut through his self-pity. Framed in the study window, he could see the two men, Chief Jones and Garfield Sumner sitting across a desk from each other. Garfield held a glass in his hand, Jones a cigar. They could have been talking about the day's baseball scores, they could have been talking about how Garfield Sumner could not possibly have murdered his wife because he was registered in a Chicago hotel at the time, and besides had no motive. Johnny dug clenched fists deep in his pockets and walked on. "If Garfield should ever find out, he'd want to kill me," Cara had said, smiling down at him, tracing with her fingertip the line of his jaw. "And I shouldn't blame him in the least," she'd said, the smiling giving away to a thoughtful sadness.

Stung by this intrusion of her marriage, he'd said, "Then how can you?" Sounding angry, feeling only young, inept.

"How not? . . ." She was sitting up then, pushing at her hair, the stray ends, with the back of her hand and looking off and away to a place where he wasn't and never had been. "Old worlds revisited, a new continent to explore, all at one and the same time. With you I feel timeless and ageless. Not young, though no one would believe that that isn't what I, what you . . . No, not young at all, but ageless."

"Are you talking about Shangri-La?"

"Heavens no. I loathe the place. Nothing ever changes there."

"Is that what I mean to you then? Change?" He at once regretted the childish pleading sound of it. She turned to him, all loving attention, sweetly grave.

"I sometimes say things that I don't mean just because they sound clever. Don't you know that about me?" He could only shake his head. There was much he didn't know about her. And now never would.

For a moment he had no idea where he was when the voice hailed him from the dark veranda. He'd simply been walking, straight ahead except when a traffic light went against him, and then he'd change course. It was a girl's voice, and in the surprised note of greeting there had been a hesitancy, too. When he stopped he realized that he was on Valence Street, staring dazedly across to the Michaels' house, and that the voice had been Bibsy's, though he couldn't see her.

"That is you, Johnny, isn't it? Johnny Merrill?"

She was the last person . . . the very last . . . he wanted to bolt and run . . . He stood rooted, helpless, trapped in the light from the street lamp. He could see her now, framed against a dimly lighted window as she came to lean across the veranda rail.

"Funny," she said, "I was just thinking about you. Wondering if you were mad at me. You must have read my thoughts." There was a hint of laughter in her voice, of relief, and he realized that to her this was no aimless coincidence. Wishing to God he had the ruthlessness to enlighten her . . . he moved slowly up the concrete walk to the veranda steps and up the steps to the veranda itself where, with a barely perceptible sigh, Bibsy settled back into the swing. He realized, letting himself down against the wicker framework of the chair next to it, that he was tired and that his legs ached from the walking, and his fingers from clenching them into fists.

"You look all in," Bibsy said. "Is that what writing does to you? Cathy says you're writing a play. What's it about?"

"People."

"Now you're making fun of me. What's it about really?" She gave a little push with her foot that set the swing in motion. She was wearing bare-toed sandals, and her toes coming out of them had a stubbed, uneven look. Like Marny's toes, only clean. Cara's feet were long and slender and as delicate as her hands.

"Is something the matter?" Bibsy said. "You've hardly said a word. Are you cross with me about something, is that why you haven't . . ." Her voice trailed off unhappily, and he could feel her looking at him, and because he knew he was going to have to do better than this, he looked back at her and smiled, feeling the muscles around his mouth move reassuringly. She was wearing her dark hair drawn up and back from her face, giving her eyes a tilted Oriental look oddly at variance with the boyish tidiness of her blouse and skirt and the jaunty "made in America" sandals.

He tried desperately to remember what it was he'd felt for her all those many months ago so that now out of that memory he might establish some means of communication, but all that he remembered was that the first time he'd seen Cara out of the context of her habitual environment . . . wife, neighbor, friend of his mother's . . . he had forgotten everything he'd ever felt before, and that from that day on . . .

"Of course I'm not cross with you," he said. "School, this play . . . time consuming. Tell me what you've been up to lately?" That was the way to do it. Talk about her. And keep talking.

"Didn't Cathy tell you? About our jobs?"

"I remember some talk this morning . . ."

"Well, we got them. At Stone's. Cathy's in lingerie; I'm in cosmetics."

"Do you think you'll stick it?"

"I'll have to. That is, if I ever expect to get to college. Don't tell Cathy though."

"Why not tell Cathy?"

"Oh, I don't know. It's more fun if she thinks we're doing it for the same reason . . . adventure, all that jazz."

"Why do you care what Cathy thinks?"

"I care what everyone thinks. Don't you remember?"

He did vaguely, something about a quarrel they'd had . . . over holding hands in public. They'd made it up in the darkened Michael hallway, only to have Mrs. Michael turn the light on, interrupting what might have been their first kiss. He supposed that even now Mrs. Michael probably sat in the room behind them reading one of those interminable religious tracts which were her sole sustenance in a life complicated by the vast discrepancy between what she was and what she wished to be.

"I can't help wanting people to approve of me," Bibsy said, mistaking his silence, "any more than you can help not caring what people think of you."

"Whatever gave you that idea?"

"It's the way you go about things. Everything. From the inside out instead of the opposite. Me, I start with the outside, and then make the inside fit. But I guess I don't make much sense, do I? . . . Would you like something cold to drink?" In one nervous motion she was out of the swing. "Some beer, perhaps?"

"Thanks, but I've got to be shoving off. I only wanted

Everybody Adored Cara

to see how you were getting along, what was new..."
The glibness of the lie shocked him. You learn fast, he thought grimly, and started toward the steps.

"I don't think you meant to come at all," Bibsy said in a small faraway voice, and he turned. She was leaning against the door, her hand behind her on the knob. "I think you just happened to be going by, and I..."

"It wasn't like that at all," he said gruffly, unable to meet her eyes. "It's just that tomorrow I've got to be fresh... writing takes a lot out of you..."

"Well, it was nice seeing you. I wish you luck with your play." Her eyes were suddenly very bright as swiftly she turned and opened the door.

On his way home he stopped off at Barny's for a beer, but the place was filled with couples looking into each other's eyes as they writhed before the juke box. It made him sick. And it made him lonely, so he drank one fast one and left. The lights in the Sumner house were off now, even the light in the second floor bathroom which Cara, being afraid of the dark, had always kept burning the night through.

He still wasn't ready to face his room and the bed that would offer him no rest. Also, there was still a light on in his parents' room, and he wasn't ready to face them either. He walked around the side of the house and climbed into his jalopy. He wasn't going anywhere. It was just a place to sit. His hand, groping along the seat edge for the matches that invariably could be found there, encountered a small slithery metal object. A chain of some sort. He turned on the ignition and held the thing under the dashboard light. It was the locket, the gold heart dangling from a tiny gold chain, that he'd given Cara for Christmas. He had bought it with money he'd got by pawning his watch and the ten dollars the *Fairless Review* had paid him for a ballad about the Alamo. Stunned, he held it cupped against his cheek for a moment, believing almost that Cara spoke to him. He could see her now, bent over the satin-lined box it had come in, the color coming and going in her cheeks as it did when she was deeply moved.

"Oh Johnny, however did you get it?"

"The poem," he said, and then because he remembered she knew what he'd got for the poem, and because he didn't want her to think it a mere ten dollar trifle, he'd added, "that and some money I'd saved."

"You know I can never wear it, don't you?"

He hadn't known. "You've so many jewels, why should anyone notice one more?"

"But a heart, Johnny, and yours. I couldn't wear it. It wouldn't be fair. Not to anyone. But it's enough for me that I have it. That you gave it to me. Is that enough for you?"

"Of course." And it was, or almost. She spoke of it often, of how tender and innocent it looked there alongside all the cold diamonds and pearls. She spoke of it often, but she never wore it. Not ever. So she couldn't have left it in his car. Not unless . . . and was that what she'd wanted to tell him the day she'd gotten him to drive her to market? The day before she died! He leaned his head back against the worn car seat and went over that day, the part of it that had Cara in it. . . .

It was his mother who had asked him to take Cara to market. Cara had called and said her car battery was dead. The request coming like that out in the open, had made him uneasy. Sensitive to Cara's every mood it didn't take much to feel in this neighborly favor-asking through proper channels a return to the old status. Her friend Lindsey's boy . . . "How are you today, Johnny? How's school?" Or could it mean that she was in some sort of trouble? With Garfield? And that that this was a cry for help. He'd wanted to believe that was the way it was but the minute he saw her he knew it wasn't. She looked sweet and pretty and unruffled and when he tried to put his hand over hers on the seat between them she drew her hand away.

"I did have a dead battery," she said matter-of-factly and his throat went dry. It was the voice she used for everyone and still in that voice she added, "But I did want to talk to you."

"You make it sound ominous," he growled hoping to discourage her. Apparently he succeeded for she was silent. But he found he couldn't leave her silence alone.

"In fact," he said, "you sound like the beginning of a 'Dear John' bit." But the growl had gone out of his voice and even to him it sounded scared. She must have thought so too because she gave him a long undecided look and turned away and stared hard out of the window.

"You are such a *child*," she murmured finally and furtively blew her nose.

At any other time he would have argued the misnomer but he felt that however ignoble her charge, he had won some sort of victory and he wanted now only to change the subject. He began at once to tell her of the progress he was making on his play and she, as always when he talked about his writing, became once more tractable and attentive, the one he thought of as "his Cara."

And that, as far as he could remember had been it. While she did her marketing he had whiled away the time in the record shop next door. Always a fatal pastime as he had ended up charging a Beethoven Sonata. That was what he and Cara had talked about on the drive home. Music. He drove her to her back door and carried in her groceries while she . . . and now he had it, while she remained for a few minutes in the car. He had thought she was waiting for him, considering saying whatever it was she'd wanted to say, so he'd played it cool . . . or so he thought at the time . . . and stayed loitering in the kitchen until he heard the car door slam. Now it came clear.

With an oath that was half-sob he stuffed the locket

into his pocket and made his way blindly across the night-black yard to the house. She had meant to give him back the locket. She had had it with her all the time. And, when he stalled her off, when he let her see how scared he was, she couldn't go through with it . . . it must have been like that, had to be like that . . . and so when she couldn't go through with it, couldn't tell him, she'd left it stuffed in the seat crack. She knew he'd find it eventually. She knew he was always taking the damned jalopy apart. But why did she want to return it?

Nothing had changed. Garfield! Garfield must have come across the locket, questioned her and then read his own dirty suspicious interpretation into what she'd told him. He found that he was trembling with rage, and there was not one damned thing he could do about it, or with it.

Bibsy leaned against the closed door listening to Johnny's departing steps echoing down the quiet, empty street. There goes nothing, she thought, and brushed at her eyes with the back of her hand.

"Elizabeth?" Her mother's voice coming from the living room held a note of remonstrance. For a moment Bibsy pretended not to hear. But it was no use. Her mother of course knew she had heard, and would in a moment come out into the hall to see what the trouble was. So she went into the living room, making up a smile as she went. Her mother was sitting under the lamp, turning the collar on one of her father's shirts, so that the shine and the worn places wouldn't show.

"Was that the Merrill boy out there?"

"Yes."

"You didn't tell me you expected him, or I'd have got out some refreshments . . ."

"I forgot to tell you. It just didn't seem that important."

"It must not have been; he certainly didn't stay long."

Her mother looked up archly from her sewing. It was a look meant to convey compatibility, to encourage confidences, but all it did was to remind Bibsy to be careful.

"I told him I was tired," she yawned elaborately.

"Good for you!" Her mother's worn face momentarily lighted. "Give him a taste of his own medicine. I always felt he was taking you much too much for granted."

"Oh, Mother! Don't be silly. We're just friends."

"I'm glad to hear that. For a while I was afraid that you were taking him much too seriously."

"Never fear," Bibsy said and started for the door.

"I don't want you getting hurt," her mother said, "and there's no reason why you should. You may not have the Merrill money or the fancy schooling, but you've got plenty to offer when the right boy comes along."

"Yes, Mother."

"For instance, that Robby Rowels. And you've so much in common . . . your music . . . such nice manners too, and a good future. He seems like a real sweet boy."

"He is a real sweet boy."

"Then why?"

She knew she shouldn't, but she couldn't help it. Her mother was always driving her to this. This spending of unrelated hurts, unrelated angers on her. "Because he's just too damned sweet, that's why. He's a pansy, a queer. He doesn't like girls. Anybody with eyes and ears can tell that."

"Oh, oh, oh." Her mother dropped her sewing and put her hand to her mouth as though she'd been struck, and around the hand her skin grew red, the red spreading inch by inch until it covered her face like a stain. "How can you talk so? How do you know so much? No nice girl . . . even if it were true, no nice girl . . ." She broke off and looked at her daughter with anxious, tear-filled eyes.

"I'm sorry." Now that it was over and done, she *was* sorry. Truly sorry, but even as she went to pat her mother's shoulder in an agony of regret, she knew she would be hurting her again in just this way. Deliberately. And for all the wrong reasons.

"Can I fix you some iced coffee before I go to bed?"

"No, thank you. Your father ought to be coming in any minute now. They're bowling Beaton's Hardware, an early game he said."

"Why is it you never go with him? It's something you could do together."

She was always trying to improve on the relationship between her parents, though she knew it did no good. They were what they were, and what they felt for each other was the sum total of this, no less, no more. They did what they could for each other.

"What on earth would I find to do in a bowling alley?" her mother said, just as she'd known she would. "We go to church together, which is far more to the point."

Upstairs in her room Bibsy didn't turn on the light. There was a candle on the table beside her bed, and this she struck a match to. By candlelight the room was almost pretty. By candlelight you weren't aware of the disparity of tastes represented . . . her mother's organdy curtains and flounced organdy bedspread . . . "A young girl should have pretty feminine things around her" . . . her own maps on the walls, studded with gaily colored pins, marking her progress around the world via the Stoningham Public Library, the office chair out of the cellar she'd insisted on because it was just the right height for the window ledges which was where she did all her studying, scorning the delicate little writing table her mother had found at an auction.

From a jewel case on the bureau she withdrew a key, and unlocking the drawer in this same writing table, she took out a leather-bound diary to which was attached a gold pencil. She placed them on the table beside the bed next to the candle and then began, slowly, methodically, to undress, hanging skirt and blouse in the closet, placing her sandals on a rack in the closet. Turning to get pajamas out of the bureau, she saw her naked reflection in the mirror, and as though she'd stumbled inadvertently into the room of a stranger, she flushed and turned quickly away and hastily scrambled into her pajamas. She pulled back the organdy spread, folding it tidily at the foot of her bed, and propping herself up on the one pillow reached for the diary. On the space allotted for June 10, she wrote: *"He came tonight. He really is insufferable. So arrogant. And self-centered. He hardly said a word. When he left I had the awful feeling I was going to start crying. I felt as though it was the end of everything. Even our being friends. But maybe I just imagined it. As he said, writing takes a lot out of you. Maybe he was just tired."*

She sighed, closed the diary, but just as she was about to blow the candle out she opened it again and wrote, *"I got a job today. From nine to five at Stone's. It pays twenty-five dollars a week."*

The next morning at breakfast, Frank Merrill read the account of the murder aloud because there was only one paper, and he assumed they were all as anxious as he to learn if there'd been any new developments. The only new development was the missing locket.

"Then that writes it off as a simple thief, doesn't it?" Lindsey said with a touch of relief.

"Not at all," her husband corrected and read on. " 'Mr. Garfield said the locket, which was of little value, was removed from a jewel case containing pearls of far greater worth which had not been touched. Chief Jones stated that the missing locket may have no bearing on the case, that Mrs. Sumner may have removed it from the case in Mr. Sumner's absence, could have worn it and misplaced or lost it. It was in order, Mr. Sumner said, to rule it out as evidence if it could be ruled out, that he is offering a five-hundred-dollar reward to anyone who can supply information leading to the recovery of the locket.'"

"Whew!" Cathy said. "And what damned fool would want five hundred dollars that bad?"

"Someone innocent and honest," her mother said, "who had found the locket somewhere and wondered who it belonged to."

"I think it very wise of Garfield to make this move," her father said. "If the locket has nothing to do with the case, the sooner they know it the better."

"Whatever they do, I do hope they'll be quick about it," Lindsey said. "I hate the feeling that someone . . ." She broke off and put down the forkful of food she'd been about to sample. Johnny, who had been listening with what he hoped appeared to be merely polite attention, suddenly pushed back his chair.

"You've hardly eaten a thing," his mother said.

"I want to get started early today."

"How on earth can you concentrate at a time like this?" Cathy said. "I can't seem to settle down to anything, and yet what is there to *do*, when you come right down to it."

"I think this might just be the day to go to the lake," Lindsey said. "All of us. We can pick up Marny and . . ."

"I'm afraid that's out of the question," her husband said. "They'll want us here. For questioning."

"Why us?" Lindsey said plaintively.

"Not only us," Frank said, "everyone that ever knew or heard of Cara . . . Don't you realize, my dear, that there is a murderer at large, and that the sooner he's caught . . . So far they've nothing to go on. No motive, no nothing, except a silly bauble that Cara may have lost herself. There will have to be questioning, a great deal of it. I for one am only too glad to help."

"Now that you put it that way . . ." Lindsey sighed.

"I still don't get all the furor over the locket," Cathy

said. "What if the murderer did take it, all it proves is that he doesn't know the first thing about jewelry."

"It does rather sound as though they're clutching at straws," her mother agreed.

"Not straws exactly." Frank hesitated and glanced at Cathy as though he weighed the discretion of what he had been going to say. Deciding probably that she was bound to hear it sooner or later he shrugged. "You see, this locket thing was in the shape of a heart."

"Fiddlesticks," said Lindsey. "I can't see any significance in that. Cara had lived half her life before she ever met Garfield. It was probably a leftover from her first marriage, or even from some high school flame. We all have them..."

"You do?" Frank exploded.

"Of course we do. Know that butterfly pin you've always thought was hideous? I wouldn't part with it for the world. I can't even remember the boy's name now, but I remember every detail about the summer he gave it to me."

"Well, I guess it's too late for that to serve as a warning to me, but I hope Johnny hears you, eh, Johnny?"

But Johnny hadn't been there for some time. He was up in his room pacing the floor, the locket in his shirt pocket burning a hole in his heart. He knew what he should do. He should take the locket into Marny's room to the window that overlooked the Sumners' back yard, and he should throw it just as far as it would go. That is what he should do if he wanted to play it smart. He should get rid of the thing. And fast. But he couldn't bring himself to do it. He got the locket out of his pocket and looked at it. He had to keep it. It was all that he had left of her that he could touch. In his closet there was a cardboard box filled with old, rejected manuscripts dating dack to the first story he'd ever written. He was twelve when he wrote it. It was about an old man and a dog. Naturally. He put the locket on the bottom of the box and the dried, wilted papers on top of it and put it back in the closet. He felt better after that. As though he'd taken a stand, though he hadn't any idea just what that stand was.

He went and sat down at his desk and stared blankly at yesterday's pages. A well-known writer had once said that a writer must build a fence around his work, a fence without gates. No gate for love, no gate for tragedy or loss. A writer, he had said, must sit inside that fence and work.

He tried to imagine the fence. Wrought iron it would have to be, with barbed wire at the top. He imagined himself inside such a fence and wrote a quarter of page of dialogue. But when he read it over, it sounded forced, empty. It was forced. It was empty. And it was going to be that way for a long time. For a long time he was going to be stuck in this room at this desk forcing emptiness. He swore and pushed the pages of the play off the desk and to the floor. Putting a clean piece of copy paper into his typewriter, he wrote:

"It was her hair that everybody talked about, but that wasn't what made him look at her that first time. He'd been seeing her for a long time without looking at her. He'd seen her coming in and out of his parents' house, coming in and out of the house next door where she lived, but it wasn't until she spoke to him that he'd really looked at her, had begun to think of her as a woman, had begun to think of himself as a man. Or that he could be. That it wasn't too far off. She'd spoken to him before, of course, and he to her. 'Good morning'; 'Good afternoon'; 'Is your mother at home?'; 'How's college going?' The usual mother's friend gambit. He'd had a quarrel with his father that day about changing his major. From Biology to English. His passion for biology had been a boy's passion that turned cold and dead in the laboratory. He'd won the victory but lost the war and was still squirming from the things his father had said to him. She'd come over somewhere near the end of it to bring his mother a recipe and must have heard snatches of it." Johnny reread what he'd written and sighing tilted back his chair and stared up at the ceiling.

While she was there it had started to rain. A nasty windblown November rain that didn't look like it wanted to stop. His mother called him into the kitchen where they'd been having coffee and asked him to find an umbrella and take her home. His mother lent her a raincoat which was much too big for her. He wasn't used to playing the gallant and was so intent on keeping the rain off her he got soaked to the skin. When they got inside, he felt like shaking himself like a dog but, still the gentleman, he stood quietly and dripped while she took off his mother's raincoat and handed it to him. "I think you'll make it," she said. Thinking she meant the trip home, he said, "Sure, and if I don't I can always swim."

"Maybe that too," she said. "I was talking about your wanting to be a writer." Her voice when she said it had a lilt to it as though she wasn't saying it for his sake, but for hers too, as though it made her happy to say it. He looked at her then, gray eyes in a small pointed face smiled back at him. And then suddenly, as though she found his look uncomfortable, she looked away. It was that look away, the shy, tremulous business of escaping from the periphery of his eyes that set his heart to pounding and turned loose a singing in his head.

"Thanks," he stammered, "thanks for thinking that."

"You're quite welcome," she said, matter-of-factly, "and thank you for keeping my powder dry. Oh, and tell Lindsey that with that recipe I always go a little light on the flour."

He hung around a minute longer dripping on her rug and waiting for that thing between them to come back into her voice, her eyes, but she held him at bay, busying herself with being once more Mrs. So and So, his mother's friend.

Before going to the office Frank stopped in next door. Mr. Sumner, the maid told him, was in his study with Mr. Lewis, his lawyer, and didn't wish to be disturbed. However, apparently hearing his voice, Garfield came to the study door and beckoned him in. Frank had always had great respect for Rufus Lewis, but for his own counsel he preferred someone a little less brilliant, a little more yielding, someone for instance like Sam Watkins, who might not be quite so spectacular in court but knew law and knew human nature and how to alleviate some of the vast discrepancies between the two.

"Rufus here has some new angles. Maybe you'd like to hear them." Garfield motioned him to a chair.

"Morning, Merrill," Lewis said, but didn't seem disposed to continue whatever discussion they'd been having.

"It's all right," Garfield prodded him. "Anything you can say to me you can say to him. Frank here is the best friend I've got."

The admission made Frank feel uncomfortably sorry for Garfield. Sorrier even than he already did. Sure they'd been partners for years, neighbors, friends of a sort, but to count as best friend a man who felt he only vaguely understood you—"Rufus," Garfield was saying, "thinks I made a mistake, putting a reward on the locket . . ."

"Not a mistake," Lewis interrupted, "just think you were hasty, that's all. Can't blame you." Turning to Frank he said, "I think he should have put a reward on any information leading to the arrest and conviction of the murderer, and I think he should have made it big."

"It's not too late for that." Frank said.

"Not too late," Lewis said, "but Garfield is balking."

"If it's the money . . ." Frank said to Garfield.

"Hell, no. You know better than that. Anything is worth hanging the fellow. I'd just like to give the police department a chance first. Link Jones seems competent and right on the ball. Once a reward for information, 'information' mind you, and that can be anything, think of the crackpots, the little old ladies who thought they saw, the big operators on the lookout for an easy buck. I think such a reward would hamper the police. This locket thing is tangible. Somebody has got to produce a given object. Somebody . . ."

"Sure, sure, it was a good idea as far as it went, but we still don't know that the locket has any bearing . . ."

"*I* know it does," Garfield said abruptly, and brought his fist down on the table edge.

"But I didn't call you in here to argue about that. All I want is advice on how to track down my wife's murderer."

"That's exactly what I'm giving you," Lewis said. "And my advice is to drop this locket angle for the time being. Concentrate on facts. Hire a detective to collect them. I could probably get Ridley to come down from New York. He's young but he's good. No histrionics. But thorough. Methodical. I really think he would be just what we need here."

"What exactly do we need here?" Garfield said, sounding dubious.

"A brief on your wife. A brief consisting of nothing but interviews with people who knew her. The butcher, the baker, your neighbor here . . ."

"No. I don't think Cara would like that. I don't think I would . . ."

"Have it your way." Abruptly Lewis stood up. "You wanted my advice, and that's it. You'd be surprised what a thoroughgoing investigation of that sort can turn up. Remember the Keeler case in Minneapolis last year?"

Garfield nodded, and Frank wondered if that had been the murder Cathy had got so wrought up about . . . a teenage girl . . .

"Well, it wasn't made public, but it was in just this way they broke that case. A friend of the girl who was interviewed told the investigator about a double date they'd been on six months earlier, a blind date. The blind date was contacted, and he told about a place they'd been where a stranger had made a pass at the girl. He'd told the stranger off and never given it another thought. The girl's murderer turned out to be the stranger, an erstwhile mental patient."

As he spoke he packed up his briefcase, and for a moment Frank thought Garfield was going to let him leave, but at the last minute at the door Garfield held out his hand.

"I'm sorry, Rufus. Just a stubborn fool, I guess. This invasion of my privacy . . . have to get used to it. Call your friend Ridley and let me know."

The findings of the inquest were published that evening in the *Stoningham Evening Press and Standard*. Bibsy, picking up the paper on the porch, read the account before taking it in to her parents. The story was headlined *INQUEST HELD IN BLUE CHIFFON DEATH*. And beneath it was a picture of Mrs. Sumner taken at the Symphony Ball of which she'd been one of the sponsors a number of years ago. Her bare shoulders looked surprisingly childlike to Bibsy who had always thought of her as the height of mature sophistication. "The verdict of the coroner's inquest into the death of Mrs. Garfield Sumner held this morning was, according to Coroner Fife, that she died of cardiac failure partially induced by a chiffon scarf placed about her neck by a person or persons as yet unknown. There was, Coroner Fife said, indication that Mrs. Sumner had taken sleeping pills but not in enough quantity to account for her death. Her husband said she often took pills to sleep.

"The late Mrs. Sumner, 'Cara' as she was known to friends and intimates, was found dead in her bed by the maid Friday morning at about eight o'clock. Her husband, the well-known architect, was on his way home from Chicago where he'd attended the Midwestern Architectural Forum.

"Mrs. Sumner before her marriage was fashion director for Corner and Lowe in New York City..."

Cathy had called Bibsy that morning to tell her that the murdered socialite they'd read about on the bus was her precious Cara. Cathy had sounded more bewildered than anything else, and when Bibsy found it hard to think of something appropriate to say, Cathy accused her of being unfeeling. And Bibsy supposed that she had been, but how go about drumming up feeling for someone you've never exchanged more than two words with. Given time, she knew she'd feel something real, but just at first all she could feel was a kind of outraged surprise that this sort of thing could happen to "nice" people.

"Who do you suppose did it?" Bibsy'd said.

"Is that all that you can think about?" Cathy cried in a choked voice and hung up. Bibsy had felt miserable. She couldn't bear to be on the outs with Cathy. It wasn't just because of the way she felt toward Cathy, which was sometimes warm and sometimes cold, but it was the way she felt about Johnny too and their home and the things they did and the way they lived. It was being cut off from all that she knew intimately of gaiety and freedom.

Having read all that she wished to read of the Sumner case... and the truth was it gave her a scared feeling in her tummy now that she'd had time to think about it... she took the paper inside and gave it to her mother. Mrs. Michael carefully extricated the sports section which she handed to her husband, and with a sigh settled back to enjoy the latest developments in Stoningham's first murder in twenty-five years. Bibsy didn't wait for her comments. She knew what they would be, the tone of them. This morning when she'd told her mother the gist of Cathy's telephone call, the expression on her mother's face had embarrassed her. "I always thought there was more to that woman than met the eye," she said. "And she's Mrs. Merrill's best friend, didn't you tell me?"

"They are neighbors."

"I distinctly remember your saying . . . but never mind. It does prove what I always say. There's more to being a lady than calling yourself one."

"How can you say she wasn't a lady?"

"Ladies," her mother said, "don't get murdered in their beds."

"Really Mother! It was probably a prowler and could have happened to anyone."

"Prowler or not, mark my words it's not a thing that would ever happen to the first Mrs. Sumner."

"I didn't know you knew her."

"I don't know her intimately, but I do know a lady when I see one!"

There was no arguing with her mother when she got on this subject, nor did Bibsy really want to. This conviction of infallibility was her mother's one defense against the petty humiliations of a life dedicated to keeping up the myth of her own refinement. It was a facet of her mother's personality which she instinctively knew must never be tampered with. If at times she must hurt her, there were lesser ways.

Cara's funeral was held the next day in the little Lutheran chapel that had been one of the first things Garfield had designed after he and Frank set up their partnership. Cara belonged to no church, but she had liked attending the Christmas and Easter services here. She had said, another of those revelations tossed out with such casual irrelevancy that only in retrospect did Lindsey quite grasp it . . . she had said, "I like coming here. It not only makes me feel closer to God but to Garfield as well."

Lindsey, sitting in the pew between Cathy and Frank, tried not to think about Cara. Johnny had flatly refused to come with them, and she was inclined in this instance to side with Frank. The boy really had been impossible about the whole ghastly business . . . cold, detached, selfish from the beginning . . . to think about Cara would be her undoing she knew . . . all the held-back tears, the held-back hysteria so near the surface . . .

The chapel was crowded and hot, the smell of roses almost suffocating. Lindsey reached for Frank's hand, felt it close firm and warm around hers, felt a wave of gratitude as intense as passion flow between them. Several rows ahead Garfield sat alone except for a half-forgotten sister of Cara's who had flown in from Canada that very morning. His beautifully tailored, stubbornly obdurate back struck her in this moment of silent communication with her husband as a reproach. Instinctively she withdrew her hand, and as the coffin was lifted from its place at the altar and slowly, ponderously carried down the chancel steps, she felt Cathy stiffen and tremble. She'd hardly given a thought to Cathy, to how all this was affecting her. There'd been so many other things . . . so many other people, and Cathy seemed always so in command of her helter-skelter life, so secure in her convictions about everything right or wrong, that she'd assumed, if indeed she'd thought about it at all, that Cathy had her secure convictions about this too.

A monstrous assumption really . . . Cathy was a bare five years removed from that skinny, long-legged, timorous thirteen-year-old who had invaded their room many a night tearfully demanding reassurance that some day she would be pretty, some day wise, some day noticed . . . and she had been enormously fond of Cara for reasons which Lindsey had never quite fathomed . . . there must be something, Lindsey pondered, that she could say, do. Perhaps someone her own age to take her mind off . . .

At Garfield's request it had fallen to Lindsey to collect the cards from the flowers after the services were over. Frank and Cathy remained behind with her to help, but Cathy looked so pale that she sent them back to the car to wait for her. The task appeared simple enough, but some overzealous florists had wired the cards as firmly as if they'd expected them to last out eternity. Twice she stuck her fingers and once tore the envelope so badly she simply removed the card from it and let the infernal thing remain, a small white flag to flutter midst the chrysanthemums in the graveyard breeze. The card she was about to stuff with the others in her bag when the signature caught her eye—*"Helen,"* and yes, it was her handwriting, precise, contained, so like the woman herself . . . *"I am so sorry"* the card said.

Lindsey wondered if it were possible that she really was sorry and for what. For Garfield's loss? Or the ruin made of her own life, it would seem now, for naught. Or was she, Lindsey, trying to read something into a perfectly conventional expression of sympathy? She must concede that she'd never really felt she knew Helen in spite of all the family get-togethers that Frank had insisted on. And she'd heard precious little about her since she moved to Hastings. Helen had made it clear that she had no wish to maintain any contacts too intimately associated with her former marriage. There had been a stubbornly loyal few who had persisted, Mike and Roweena Hayes, for instance. In fact after years of never knowing what to say to Roweena when they met at parties, at the supermarket, it had given Lindsey a point of contact. "What do you hear from Helen?" she could always say. She tried to remember now what some of Roweena's replies had been but could not. For the most part they'd been as dull as Roweena herself and always delivered with a slightly reproachful air. Undoubtedly deserved, Lindsey mused now, gazing down at the inscrutable little white card. There were undoubtedly ways in which she could have been nicer to Helen before the divorce and afterward. If she'd wanted to. And if Helen had let her.

Writing furiously against the silence of the house, against the knowledge of where everyone was, against the thought of a beflowered coffin toted, gaped at, chanted over, toted, gaped at, lowered, lowered ... Johnny wrote: "Are you in love with me?" He was always asking her that even though he knew it hurt her. He didn't ask her to hurt her. He asked her because he kept thinking that someday, sometime the answer would be different. It never was. "Are you in love with me?"

"I love you. Isn't that better?"

"How better?"

"Kinder. More durable."

"I don't believe you. I think you are in love with me. I think you've got some crazy notion about not wanting to tie me down."

"I've got a lot of crazy notions, but that's not one of them." Her laughter was for herself, about herself.

"Are you in love with your husband?"

"You mustn't do this, Johnny. To either of us."

"Are you?"

"I don't think I've ever been in love. Not the way you mean."

"How do I mean?"

"Blind, heedless, young..."

"But you've said I make you feel young."

"Not young. Ageless."

"And how does *he* make you feel?" Pain made him irresponsible.

She'd been sitting on the pier's edge making rivulet patterns in the water with her toes, but she leaped up then. He'd never seen her angry before. Or wounded. The two made a shambles of her face. "In case you didn't hear that sharp clicking noise," she said levelly, "it was my mind closing. Now shall we take that swim or shall we go?"

They took that swim. They swam out to the raft and back, and when they finally stood dripping on the dock, everything was all right again. She was Cara and the way she was, and he didn't want her any different. Not in any way. And he told her so. Everything was all right. But when he let her out down the road where she'd left her car, he saw that she was crying. Not much. Just a few tears wobbling down her cheek and no noise. "Don't ask me why," she said. "I don't know." She pushed a smile through the mist for his benefit and blew him a kiss.

Downstairs he heard the screen door slam and voices. So they were back. Voices and pitched a little higher than the others, Marny's voice. "Was it a nice funeral?" He crossed his arms over the typewriter, and his head fell against them, and he began to cry, great lunging sobs. The more he told himself to stop, you fool, they'll hear you, you fool, the worse it got. He heard the footsteps mounting the stairs, but there was nothing he could do about those either. When he looked up his father had already opened the door. His father was looking at him as though he were a kid again. The way he'd used to look at him sometimes when he was a kid and got hurt. Only he wasn't a kid, and his father looked scared.

"God damn it," Johnny got up, kicked back his chair. "It's this damned play! It doesn't move. The goddamned thing doesn't move! I'll *never* be a writer. God knows why I ever thought I would!"

His father's face crumpled into a grin. "Is that all?" He came into the room, flung an arm across his shoulders. "For a minute there I thought you'd gone stir crazy. Shut off up here by yourself day in and day out . . . it's enough to give any healthy young man the howling fits."

"I guess you're right," Johnny rubbed at his eyes with his sleeve. The sheet on which he'd been writing was still propped in the typewriter where his father, if his eyes should wander, could read it. He ducked his father's arm and tore the sheet out, crumpling it in his fist.

"Oh, now, I don't know," his father said. "Maybe it's not all that bad."

"Maybe not," he muttered and dived for the cigarettes that were on the desk. Lighted one, inhaling deeply.

"But it's time you came up for air. Get on a clean shirt

Everybody Adored Cara 69

and come downstairs. Thought we might have a highball before dinner. We can all use some cheering up."

"Yes, sir," he said, hating himself for the "sir," a relic from a meek and subservient childhood.

"See you in a few minutes then," his father said.

He heard his father greet his mother on the second landing . . . Had she been there all along? Hearing it all? His father's voice was low when he spoke to her, but he strained to hear it, and he succeeded. "It's all right," his father said. "The boy's quite all right. Come to his senses at last I do believe."

By the next day "The Blue Chiffon Murder," as it had come to be known in the papers, was already relegated to section B with the small and discouraging headline, No Suspect as Yet.

Lindsey, having got Cathy off to her first day at Stone's, left the others at the breakfast table to fend for themselves and took the newspaper and a pot of coffee back to bed. She read the brief paragraph beneath the headline with weary indifference. She was beginning, after the emotional intensity of the past few days, to hope almost that Cara's murderer might never be caught so that they could put the ghastly business out of their minds and get back to normal. At this moment the vague unreality of a murderer "at large" was far less disturbing than the thought of some crazed face staring at them from the front pages some morning, of having to get used, all over again, to the notion of violence. She turned to the Woman's page to see what had been accomplished by the Stoningham library committee in her absence. Well, they'd voted down the current events course which had been one of her pet projects and had voted in the new ruling on lost books which she'd fought tooth and nail! Which, she supposed philosophically, made her, if she believed in democracy, absolutely indispensable to the Stoningham library committee. For solace she turned to the more frivolous reporting of one Jennifer Wren whose weekly column "Ladies, Ladies" was read by every woman in Stoningham, Lindsey was sure, though she could count on one hand the number that admitted it. The ladies of Stoningham did not consider Miss Wren qualified to judge what and whom constituted Stoningham's social life. There was today a chatty write-up of Miss Wren's encounter with Mrs. P. W. "Budgy" Smoak who planned a trip to Europe, a story about one of the June brides and, popping out at Lindsey like a jack-in-the-box . . . "The tea for Mrs. Helen Sumner who was in town this week has been canceled, and Mrs. Sumner has returned to Hastings. She was, as you may remember, at one time married to the architect Garfield Sumner whose second wife died here so tragically last week. The tea was canceled, according to Mrs. Hayes, her would-be hostess, 'in the interest of good taste.' A gallant gesture, methinks," thought Jennifer Wren, and Lindsey somewhat agreed, though it seemed rather too bad and a trifle theatrical.

Frank came into the room to kiss her goodbye and change to another tie. This one was wrinkled. "Why don't you just stay there all day," he said, eying with satisfaction her robed self on the paper-strewn bed. "You need a breather."

"We all do," she sighed. "Any chance of a trip when things quiet down?"

"They aren't going to quiet down any time soon. I figured once the funeral was over, Garfield would want to come back to the office . . . take his mind off . . . but last night he asked me to take over. Indefinitely. Says he can't think about anything else until this thing is solved."

"Doesn't he realize it may never be?"

"I can't believe that," he leaned and kissed her. "Take it easy and stop worrying about Johnny. He's going to be all right. I caught him sneaking a look at the want ads this morning. Maybe a little talking to from you right now might clinch the business. Anyhow, it's worth a try."

But she wasn't at all sure she wanted to "clinch the business." She lay thinking about this after Frank had gone. There had been something in Johnny's outburst the evening before that had frightened her, had held her rooted to the spot, unable to go to him. By the time she was freed of her first paralyzing distress, Frank was already with him, and she'd felt it best to leave them alone. Give father and son a chance. But she'd not been satisfied with the explanation Johnny gave his father. Johnny had his frailties, but quitting wasn't among them. Nor could she believe the moment's discouragement would bring on so abandoned an agony. She would have a talk with him, but it wouldn't be the one Frank expected. Just what it would be she didn't know. Johnny had been awfully hard to reach of late.

Cathy and Bibsy sat on stools at the lunch counter of Stone's department store eating their first earned meal—two Cokes, two Nabs, and one salad which they divided between them.

"My feet hurt, do yours?" Bibsy sloughed off her pumps and sighed.

"I haven't even thought about my feet, I've been so busy. Honestly Bibsy, I don't know when I've had so much fun . . . the people you meet . . . there was one little man that stood around blushing and stammering for five whole minutes before he got it out that he wanted a red nylon slip 'for my wife, of course,' he said. I could hardly keep a straight face. And then there was the woman that wanted 'something that don't show through' to sleep in. If Johnny wants to write, this is where he ought to be and not stuck up in that hot little room dreaming up plots." Thinking of Johnny her eyes clouded for a moment. She started to tell Bibsy about Johnny's crying jag but found it was something she couldn't easily talk about.

"Do you think Johnny has changed lately?" Bibsy was

saying. "I mean, do you think he's in love or anything like that?"

"I'd be the last to know. He never talks to me about anything any more."

"That's just what I mean," Bibsy said and shrugged, but Cathy missed the shrug. A young man had just moved onto the empty stool beside her, a young man with sandy porcupine hair, a stubborn chin, and an unexpectedly warm smile. The smile was for the waitress from whom he was ordering a cup of coffee. Otherwise Cathy wouldn't be watching him. She wasn't in the habit of watching young men. She preferred that they watch her. She needed the security of that. But this young man . . . and he wasn't so young at that . . . commanded attention. There was an air about him of urgency, of places to go and things to do. "Strong, please, and hot," he said to the waitress, and there was that same quality in his voice that she found in his face. As though everything mattered. A cup of coffee. The waitress. She wished . . . but that was ridiculous. Flushing, she turned her attention back to Bibsy, or tried to, but she couldn't remember what they'd been talking about, nor could she think of anything to say. To the left of her the young man set his cup down with a resounding clink, bent to retrieve a briefcase from the floor at Cathy's feet and departed.

To Bibsy, Cathy, finding her tongue, said, "I don't believe in love at first sight. Do you?"

Tom Ridley, revived by the cup of coffee, found the men's wear and purchased half a dozen shirts. He always forgot something when he was called out of town in a hurry. While he waited for the shirts to be wrapped, he looked about for a pay phone and, seeing none, had to give up and ask the clerk. "Fourth floor," the man said, and added in a singsong voice as though he'd made the recitation more times than he wished: "Used to be first floor, but too many people from outside took advantage. Got to be a nuisance."

Everybody Adored Cara

Tom decided to overlook the formality of a telephone call and go direct to the Sumner home. It shouldn't be too hard to locate . . . in the Wingate area, Dorchester Road . . . he'd been to Stoningham before. But under entirely different circumstances. There'd been a girl who lived here. For a while his girl. But then she'd married someone else. Married someone else and had a baby and died of it. All he could think when he'd heard about it was that if it had been their baby it wouldn't have happened.

It shouldn't be hard to locate, and Mr. Sumner was expecting him. The little car the rental service had had at the airport for him drove smoothly. He was almost tempted to go the long way around and through the street where the girl had lived, but what was the percentage in that?

His first impression of the Sumner house was that for an architect's home it showed little imagination. A large white brick edifice with green blinds and green mansard roof, it looked as if it had been built from plans culled from one of the women's homemaking magazines. However, once inside the picture changed. Waiting in the wide hall for the maid to make his presence known, he looked with pleasure at the paintings hanging in the large rooms to his left and right, at the liberal use of bright solid colors contrasting in such a way as to add all sorts of unexpected shapes and dimensions. Someone, he decided, not only had imagination but daring.

That someone, he surmised, watching Garfield walk toward him down the stairs, was not Mr. Sumner. "Correct" was the first word that came to his mind. His bearing, his tailored black suit, the upright graying hair at his temple, his handshake bespoke an austere restraint.

"I should have telephoned," Tom said, "but . . ."

"Quite all right," Sumner cut him off. "Gather you had no trouble finding the place." As he spoke he turned and moved toward the rear of the house. Because it seemed indicated, Tom followed him. "We can talk with less likelihood of being interrupted in here." He opened a door to the right of the stairs and waited for Tom to precede him. This room was a study and bore little relationship to the part of the house Tom had already seen. Gray walls on which hung a hunting print, a seascape, and a large photograph of a woman with light blond hair who smiled. In the center of the room was a broad heavy desk with a glass top and imprisoned beneath the glass, the blueprint of what appeared to be a church and a gold-embossed manuscript inscribed to Garfield Sumner on which was attached a blue ribbon. Mr. Sumner seated himself in the swivel chair on the far side of the desk and indicated a chair across the desk for Tom.

"Have you seen Rufus Lewis since you got here?" Sumner asked, and at Tom's negative reply said, "Good. After all, it is I who am paying you. Too many cooks, you know . . . Now I've drawn up a list of names. Friends of Ca . . . of Mrs. Sumner's who saw her or contacted her at some time during the last few days of her life. I gather your method is to question these people in the hope of building some sort of a picture . . . but I want you to remember that for the most part these are friends of ours and must be treated with deference and consideration. Right?"

"Of course," Tom said.

"Here is the list then." He shoved a paper across the desk. "How long do you think it will take?"

Dubiously Tom scanned the half dozen or so names. "I'm afraid, sir, Mr. Lewis didn't make my procedure quite clear. It's not so much that I want to build a picture of the few days leading up to the tragedy as that I want, must, in fact, build a picture of your wife herself."

"Well now," Mr. Sumner said, "that should be easy enough . . . though I can't see what bearing—still, that's your field, not mine . . . Who could give you a clearer picture than I, her husband? Fire away!" He leaned back, arms behind his head. "Color of eyes, gray. Hair blond.

Most people didn't believe it was real, but it was. Small frame. Slight limp." He paused, sighed. "Or is all this extraneous?"

"Not entirely." Tom got out a pocket-sized notebook and balanced it on his knee.

"Perhaps you have a set of questions you like to ask?"

"No. Different questions for different people."

"Well, a set of questions for husbands then?"

"I'd rather you'd just tell me. What she was like, the things she liked to do, the kind of people she liked . . . Anything that comes to mind." As soon as he'd said it he wished he hadn't. Most people, he'd found, liked to talk about the deceased and especially to a stranger. A form of release. But Mr. Sumner, grown suddenly pale, was not most people, and he should have guessed this. Gone slower.

"Anything that comes to mind, be damned!" he said. "This is my wife we're talking about. You ask the questions, and I'll answer them. *If* I see fit."

"Right," Tom conceded, flushing. Cleared his throat. "What were your wife's hobbies?"

"She had no hobbies."

"Her interests then? Did she like to read? Garden? Play bridge? Listen to music?"

"All these things. She had a full life. No time for hobbies."

"Did she have many friends?"

"Everyone adored her. She had a way with people. Everyone. Our servants, our neighbors."

"How about family?"

"A sister. She's here with me now. Came for the funeral. But they weren't very close, not since they were children. Time, distance . . . people change. She wouldn't be of any help to you."

"Who then?"

"Our neighbors, the Merrills. And of course there is the business of the locket. I suppose Lewis told you."

"That you believed a locket had been stolen on that night..."

"Believed! I know," Sumner interrupted angrily. "Maybe not that night, but sometime in the few days that I was away. At any rate, it is a coincidence that I feel Lewis and the police are taking far too lightly."

"I gather it was of no particular value except to Mrs. Sumner."

"Still I think they treat the matter far too lightly..." His voice trailed off and Tom changed the subject.

"I take it you and your wife were very close."

"Anyone can tell you that."

"Did she belong to any clubs, any civic organizations?"

"She wasn't a joiner, if that's what you mean. Husband and home came first. But people were always asking her to help with this and that . . . she was on the library board and once a year helped with the May Day pageant in the schools . . . had a real flair for that kind of thing, and once in a while she'd get steamed up about something and start a crusade, but she'd lose interest as soon as she got things going and turn it over to someone else. As I said, she just wasn't a joiner."

"I see." Tom pretended to scribble in his notebook. It had the desired effect. Sumner fiddled nervously with his watch chain.

"I guess that covers it," Sumner said.

Tom, still pretending to write, said nothing.

"The first time I saw her," Sumner said, "was at a meeting in New York, a kind of architectural forum to which the public was invited. She came. She was a fashion designer in those days. She believed all the functional arts were related, or should be—architecture, fashion, interior decorating . . . I was sitting at the speaker's table where I got a pretty good view of everyone. She was in the eighth row back. I counted them. Eight rows back and six people in. Like putting a pin in the important spot on a map. After the discussion was over, I went looking for her. As luck would have it, when I found her she was talking to a couple I knew slightly. They introduced us. She smiled at me, and I knew I'd been right about her. I was halfway back to Stoningham before I realized I didn't even know if she was married or not. I called her from the Stoningham station and asked her." Suddenly he broke off and, looking at Tom as though he were just remembering that he was there, he said, "Just what in the devil are you writing in that notebook?"

"A list of the people I'd like to talk to." Tom said and shoved the book across the desk to him.

"The servants," Sumner read aloud, and nodded approvingly, "the sister . . . well, you'll just be wasting your time, but that's your problem; Mr. and Mrs. Merrill . . . good enough, but I also suggest you talk to the children. Cara was very fond of them and they of her. Out of the mouths of babes and sucklings . . ." he quoted absently, and suddenly brought the book down onto the desk with an angry thump. "Now see here. I want my first wife kept out of this. She never laid eyes on Cara in her life. There's no purpose to be served, none whatsoever . . ."

"I'll have to be the judge of that," Tom said quietly, firmly, but he felt no such command of the situation.

"I thought you wanted a picture of my wife. Well, I've just given you one, and I'm sure everyone on this list here will corroborate me, but there is nothing Helen can tell you of any value to you or this case. I tell you the two women never met. I want Helen left out of it. She's not in it and never has been."

Maybe he was right, but that was no longer important. It always came with every client. The point when it had to be decided who was in charge. "In that case," Tom stood up, "we're wasting each other's time, Mr. Sumner. Architecture is your field, detection is mine. I have to run my own business in my own way. Just as you do."

He waited for Sumner to make up his mind, and in those few moments felt he learned more about the man than he had during the entire interview. He was a man not used to being crossed, that was obvious, but he also had respect for those that dared to try it. He was also a man not given to quick decisions. And when he was uncertain his right eyelid quivered.

"This wasn't my idea," he said finally. "It was Lewis got me into it. But now that we've gone this far," he shrugged, "I only hope you know what you're doing."

"Aye, aye, sir," Tom grinned, but the grin got no response from Sumner who only continued to watch him coldly as he retrieved his notebook. This wasn't, Tom conceded, going to be the pleasantest assignment he'd ever had, but after all the man's wife had been murdered. He mustn't expect him to be too rational.

"I'll keep in touch," he said.

For answer, Sumner nodded.

Next door Link Jones was talking to Marny, or trying to. Marny was enjoying the occasion much too much to want to hurry it. By pretending it wasn't Cara they were talking about but someone else entirely, she could be the little girl she'd seen so often on television in one form or another. The little girl on whom everything hinged, the little girl who got wheedled and fed ice cream cones and in general was treated like a princess because she "knew something."

When her mother had told her that the chief of police wished to speak to her, Marny had tied a pink ribbon in her hair and would have changed her dress had her mother not been so impatient. He was sitting in the living room, and he didn't look nearly as at ease as she thought he should. Only for a moment when her mother left the room . . . she hadn't expected to be alone with him . . . did she have a small trembling in her tummy. But he, on the contrary, seemed much more comfortable with her mother gone, much more like the way a chief of police should be, and as soon as he said, "I hear you're a satellite hunter," everything was all right and the way she'd imagined it would be. She guessed he was going to ask her about seeing Cara go out the night before she died, or why else would he be talking about satellites. And if that was all, it wouldn't take very long, so she told him about her telescope and the time she'd seen a flying saucer and asked him if he had any children her age. He said he had them all ages, and she asked him what their names were. He started to tell her, but right in the middle stopped and got red in the face and said, "Look, little girl, your mother says you were satellite hunting Thursday night in your window. Is that right?"

"I think it was Thursday."

"The night before Mrs. Sumner, er, died."

"Yes, that was the night."

"Have you any idea what time it was?"

Marny shook her head. "It was after bedtime. Way after."

"Was anyone else up?"

"I think so. I can usually tell when I'm the only one. The house feels scary."

"Did you see any satellites?"

"No."

"Did you see anyone?"

"Yes, I saw Cara coming out of her back door."

"Where did she go?"

"She got into her car and drove off."

"Did you hear her come back?"

"No. I went to sleep."

"You're sure it was Ca . . . Mrs. Sumner you saw."

"Oh, yes."

"It was dark. How could you tell?"

"There was a light on."

"On the back steps or inside?"

"I don't know, but there was a light on somewhere, or else I wouldn't have seen."

"Did you see what she had on, what she was wearing?"

Scowling, Marny considered this, and then she remembered the dress lying crumpled beside Cara's bed the next morning. "She was wearing a green dress with turtle doves on it."

"That figures," Chief Jones said. "And now maybe if your mother will let us, you can show me this window."

"My room's not very picked up," she flushed.

"You forget," Chief Jones said. "I've got a house full of rooms just like that."

After Chief Jones left, Marny felt let down and bored. As always when she felt this way she mosied into the kitchen in search of something to eat. But her mother, busy planning dinner with Tina, shooed her out. Disconsolately she climbed the stairs. The door to Johnny's room was open, which usually meant he wasn't there. Tentatively she knocked, and when she got no answer she tiptoed in. He kept a carton of chocolate bars hidden away to nibble on while he worked. Suspecting her, he was always changing their hiding place, but she managed usually to find it. She began today by looking in the place where they'd last been. This meant dragging a chair over to the closet and standing on it to reach the upper shelf. But they were not on top of the box of discarded manuscripts, nor anywhere that she could see. Gingerly she ran her hand under the papers the box contained. Her fingers encountered something that felt like a small chain. She pulled it out to look at it, and just then heard the front door slam and Johnny's footstep on the stair. In her panic the chain, a necklace it was with a gold heart attached, slipped out of her hand and fell to the floor. If she tried to put it back she'd never make it. She darted down from the chair, snatched the necklace up, pocketed it, closed the closet door, replaced the chair and scrambled out of his room and into her own before Johnny had turned the corner of the landing.

She took the locket over to the window to look at it.

He must be planning to give it to someone, but she couldn't imagine who. The heart had no name, no initials on it. Just a heart. And when she opened it there was nothing inside. She wished now that she'd just left it there and let him think anything he wanted to. At least he wouldn't think she was a jewel thief. She'd have to get it back in that box. Watch her chance and get it back. Soon. Before he missed it. Flushed with anxiety she scurried about her room looking for a place to hide it until she could return it, trying this place and that, rejecting them all. Perhaps her pocket was the best spot after all. Right there with her so that the moment she saw her chance she could use it.

Frank got home just as Lindsey was setting the table. He looked tired, and he eyed the extra place settings with ill-feigned displeasure.

"What's this? A banquet?" He was not really averse to guests if he had been properly prepared beforehand, but he hated being taken by surprise.

"Just Garfield and Cara's sister. Her name, by the way, is Marjorie, Marjorie Gould, but I still haven't been able to find out if it's Miss or Mrs. Perhaps you can." She walked around the table to give him a placating kiss. "I only thought of it this morning. She's leaving tomorrow, and I felt I should do something..."

"I suppose you know you've set eight places."

"That's for Bibsy. She's spending the night. I felt that Cathy needed distracting."

"After a day behind a counter at Stone's, I'd think all she'd need was a bed."

"Perhaps it was a mistake, but Cathy's been rather morose and withdrawn..."

"Did you have that talk with Johnny?"

That talk! As though it were some specific speech, complete with jotted notes beforehand. "No," she said crossly. "As a matter of fact I've hardly seen him all day. In and out and restless as a gnat."

"No writing?"

"Not that I know of."

"Splendid!"

Cathy, looking far from morose or withdrawn, burst into the room. "It's been the most marvelous day!" She kicked off her shoes and, leaning over, picked them up. "There's something absolutely other-worldly about the smell of a department store. All those perfumes and powders and silks and laces. I kept expecting an orchestra to tune up and a curtain to roll back."

"I hope the smell lasts," Frank grinned.

"Where's Bibsy?" Lindsey said.

"She'll be along. Wanted to freshen up before she came. I told her Johnny would pick her up in a little while. Now all I've got to worry about is will he . . ."

"Will he what?" Johnny spoke from the doorway. He was wearing jeans and a grease-spattered shirt and had probably, Lindsey surmised, been working on that derelict car of his. He was a poor mechanic, but in times of acute stress he was apt, Lindsey had learned, to turn to the innards of a motor, swearing and fuming at his and its inadequacies.

"Oh dear," Cathy sighed. "I was going to try to lead up to it subtly. Bibsy's coming for the night. I told her you'd get her."

"Sorry, no dice. My car is all apart . . . carburetor . . ." he lied.

"You may take mine," Lindsey said firmly.

Johnny took his time in the shower. There was something about the needle-hot massage against his spine that was, he reflected, related to the compellingly soothing touch of a woman. Related but in no way like Cara's touch had been . . . but he must not think of Cara. He had made that rule this afternoon. He had made it at three-fifteen P.M. and had stuck to it until whatever time it was now. It was a good rule, but it would take practice. No more of those dead give-away scenes like the one he'd thrown yesterday. If the old man had had an ounce of intuition. Or was that the word? Understanding maybe. Never thought he'd be glad of that. Grateful for that. But still he didn't like the little sly brooding look his mother had had all day every time she looked at him. That was one reason why he mustn't think about Cara. It would begin to show. The other reason was that bastard her husband. Thinking about Cara made him want to kill him.

The evening was warm, he only half-dried himself. He started to put on slacks and an open-neck shirt, and then he remembered that the dining-room table had had a crowded look that just Bibsy wouldn't account for. Swearing under his breath he exchanged the shirt for collar, tie, and sports jacket, bemoaning those days past when he and Cathy were served an early supper in the kitchen whenever there were guests.

He had thought of course that Cathy would ride along with him to fetch Bibsy, but apparently she had no such intention. He wished Cathy would knock off this naïve matchmaking. Sometime he'd tell her. Sometime he'd tell her that while it was no skin off his back, it wasn't fair to Bibsy.

He hoped Bibsy would be ready. Five minutes alone with that mother of hers would finish him. She was ready. And waiting. In the swing, and he guessed from the quick way she came to meet him, and the "Good night, Mother" tossed firmly over her shoulder into the room beyond the window, that she knew how he felt about her mother. Suddenly it hurt him for her that this was so, and taking her overnight bag from her, he let his fingers touch her wrist in recognition. And realized with an almost resentful surprise, that he was beginning to feel again. That is outside of himself. He looked at Bibsy blankly, wonderingly, but he wasn't really thinking about her any more. He was thinking that he mustn't let this thing happen, this feeling outside himself, this awareness of present people, present things. He must not think of Cara, but he must not lose her either.

To Bibsy he said, "What in the devil have you got in this suitcase, The Great Books series?"

After the rather unsatisfactory meeting with Garfield Sumner, Tom Ridley checked in at the Stoningham Inn. There were several motels in the city and a hotel, but he always stayed at an inn when possible, liking the sense of companionship and comfort the title evoked, though in actual fact he had never found either in any marked degree no matter where he stayed. However, this one had the advantage of being on the outskirts of the town and not too far from the Sumner home. And his room on the second floor was, except for some dismal flower prints on the walls, attractive enough. The two windows looked out on a lawn brightly patched with umbrella-shaded tables and wrought-iron chairs. He unwrapped his new shirts and placed them in the bureau drawer. From his briefcase he took his razor, a comb, a deodorant stick, a tin of talcum powder, tooth brush and paste, and placed them on a shelf in the bathroom. He then put the book he'd brought, a paperback edition of *Moby Dick,* on the table beside the bed, but this was all automatic. His thoughts were back in the study at the Sumner house, because in a moment he was going to have to get down to what he called "spade work." Taking a heavy black notebook out of the now almost empty briefcase, he sat down at the desk. At the top of the first page he wrote *Cara Sumner,* and below it and to the left *Garfield Sumner,* and then rapidly, almost as though he were receiving dictation and afraid to hesitate, he wrote: *Arrogant, proud, possessive, reserved. Love at first sight angle hard to swallow, but Cara must have packed a wallop. Sumner was not a man to compose love stories out of his head. According to G.S., his wife was an extremely attractive woman with few sustaining interests outside the home and no close friends. A woman sublimely and happily absorbed in her husband!*

Abruptly his pen stopped moving. Was that really all he'd gotten out of the man? He scowled, pulling at his ear, reread the all too brief notes. He'd planned to put off any further interviews until morning, but at this rate he'd be stuck here forever. He got up and hunted a telephone book. Merrill, Frank, Dorchester Road. A woman answered. Or rather a girl. No woman would inject so much of herself into the mere answering of a telephone.

He said, "I'm Tom Ridley, and I'd like to speak to Mr. Merrill if he's there."

There was a breathless pause at the other end and then she said, "Would you say that again?"

He repeated what he'd said. She seemed to go on listening for a moment after he'd finished and then said in a small, preoccupied voice that she'd see. In a moment Merrill answered. Yes, he'd heard that he'd come down on the Sumner case. He wanted to cooperate in any way. They all did, but the fact was . . . he broke off and said, "Just a minute. I'll let you talk to my wife."

This time the wait was interminable. Were it not for the distant background sound of voices he would have believed they'd been disconnected. He was about to give up anyway when suddenly a voice said, "This is Lindsey Merrill."

He explained again who he was and what he wished of them. He said that of course if it wasn't convenient this evening, and she interrupted him to say that as a matter of fact it wasn't, that they had guests, Mr. Sumner, in fact, and his sister-in-law, but still they did want to help and she realized that the sooner and then interrupted herself to say, "I suppose actually I'm procrastinating. We should be through dinner at about eight. Supposing you come then."

After he hung up he called room service and ordered a

scotch and soda and, taking off his coat and shirt in preparation for a quick shower, glanced over the list of names he'd made that afternoon in Sumner's study. There were three Merrill children. It had not been necessary for Sumner to suggest he talk with them. Children he had found were usually his best source of material, the younger the better, but whatever the age up until twenty they were by and large forthright, full of ideas, of opinions, and nine times out of ten presented him with a far clearer picture than their more inhibited elders. He hoped this would hold now. His interview with Sumner had left him with a creeping sense of failure and a brand-new set of doubts about what he fondly thought of as "The Ridley Method."

Bibsy, always alert to the slightest change of aspect in Johnny, was aware as they entered the Merrill living room that he had in some way been surprised, caught off guard. They had on the ride over been talking about a book Bibsy had just read about dolphins and all that they had in common with humans. "Only," summed up Bibsy, "they are much nicer. Trusting and kind and this marvelous sense of humor." This as they walked through the front door and down the hall, and at the living-room door Johnny was saying, "I never did like that monkey tie-in. I'd much rather be related to a dolphin." He was saying that, and he finished, but the last few words seemed to float off by themselves, and his face wore the look of someone who has just entered a room without knocking and wishes to go back and do it differently, only of course he didn't. He walked on into the room, and it seemed to Bibsy he'd completely forgotten her. She remained uncertainly in the doorway until Cathy, who was sitting next to a plump pretty woman, saw her and came to her rescue. She hadn't known there would be guests and wished now she'd worn something more formal than the tailored blue linen which Johnny had once long ago admired. Wished almost that she'd not come at all. She was at her absolute worst with strangers, stiff and prim and unyielding. Cathy, leading her across the room, planted her in front of the woman she'd just been talking to. "Mrs. Gould," Cathy said, "this is Bibsy Michael. She and I have just wound up our first day at Stone's department store . . . what a lark! Bibsy, Mrs. Gould is Cara's sister from Canada . . . oh, and this"—as a tall man who looked vaguely familiar got to his feet in the chair next to Mrs. Gould's—"is Mr. Sumner"—and after only the briefest hesitation—"Daddy's partner."

"Pleased to meet you," Bibsy said and flushed. She'd known for years the proper greeting was "How do you do," but always in times of stress she blurted out the other more familiar one. However, this time it didn't seem to matter. Mr. Sumner appeared to have heard neither Cathy's introduction nor her own stupid acknowledgment. He was swishing the ice in his empty glass around and looking intently at something or someone on the other side of the room.

"Come and help me with the hors d'oeuvres," Cathy said into her ear. "I've simply got to tell you something."

But once they were in the kitchen Cathy became all at once reluctant. "I'm really not sure I want to tell you . . . it's too silly actually." Her head disappeared into the icebox, emerged. "I hope this cheese isn't moldy. It's all there is . . ."

"The suspense is killing me," Bibsy said. "Out with it!"

"If only I'd asked him to say, 'Strong, please, and hot,' then I'd have known one way or another." She wandered to the cabinet in search of a plate for the cheese and then stood trying to remember what it was she looked for. "You must promise not to laugh, Bibsy, even if it turns out I'm imagining things, *especially* then. Do you remember that man when we were having lunch today? The one on my left with the stubborn jaw and the voice that sounded as though he liked being alive . . . do you remember?"

"No," Bibsy said, "I don't."

"I don't see how you could help . . . well, he was there. He ordered a cup of coffee. And then he drank it. And then he left. And I thought, well, that's that. But do you know what? This is the incredible part, the really unbelievable thing. I think he's the detective Mr. Sumner hired from New York. I honestly think that's who he is and he's coming here, to this house, tonight."

"What makes you think so?" Bibsy gouged open a bag of potato chips with a faintly tinted nail.

"Mother said so. He wants to talk to all of us. *All* of us, Bibs."

"But how do you know it's this character you saw, one and the same?"

"Because I answered the phone . . . his voice . . . I made him repeat his name, and well, I just don't see how two men could have the exact same identical way of sounding. Do you?"

"I've never seen you quite like this," Bibsy said wonderingly. "Not over a man anyway. Better take it easy. Even if it is one and the same, how do you know he's not married, etcetera?"

"I knew I shouldn't have told you," Cathy said disconsolately, and reaching into the cupboard got out a plate and placed the cheese on it.

In the living room Johnny made short work of his first drink and mixed himself another. It was amazing the composure to be got from a bottle. He had known that eventually he'd come face to face with Garfield Sumner, but he hadn't expected it tonight, and he hadn't expected that fishy stare that even now he could feel boring through his back like a twisting knife. The bastard. He was sure now. Only one person could have put that locket in his car. And for only one reason. He was about to mix his third drink when he felt his mother's hand on his wrist, light, beseeching. The eyes she raised to his were puzzled, anxious. Slowly, deliberately he put his glass down. She was right. She didn't know how right she was.

"The line between composure," he said to her, "and decomposure is a narrow one, is it not, Mother dear?" But she hadn't lingered to see if her wish had been adhered to. That was like her. And still he felt those eyes on him and wheeled to face them down, but Sumner was talking to his father, his back half-turned. It was Marny who was watching him, hand in pocket, eyes narrowed, she inched toward the door. Probably been into his candy again or was planning to while he was out of his room. Some day he'd really shake her up, leave it right out in plain sight. Marny, not looking at him now, eased out the door. He gave her a small head start. And then he went after her, his voice catching her just as she hit the first landing. "I know what you're up to!" She turned, startled beyond anything he'd meant to do, and suddenly burst into tears.

"Hey there." He took the steps three at a time. "It's just a game. You know I don't really care about the candy. Don't you know that?" She nodded, her hand still clutching at her pocket, tearful eyes not meeting his. He dabbed at the evasive eyes with a handkerchief. "You mustn't be scared of me. Oh, sure, I know I blow up sometimes but . . ." He broke off. But what? The way she'd looked at him down there . . . had she read the murder in his heart, the hate . . . kids had a way of . . . "I'm not really such a bad guy, am I?" He was shocked at the pleading in his voice, the doubt. Marny shook her head and brought her hand out of her pocket and opened the tightly folded fingers for him to see the locket that lay coiled in the small padded palm.

"I didn't steal it. It just dropped, and I didn't have time to put it back. I was trying to put it back."

"Oh my God!" He plucked up the locket, pocketed it. But he shouldn't have said that, done that. Casual was the thing. Cool. "Thanks, kid." He sounded anything but cool.

"Then you're not mad at me?"

"No, not mad." Distractedly he patted the top of her head. "But a man likes a little privacy, you know. Likes to feel that his room, his own room . . ." Should he tell her this must be a secret between them? Or play it down? She wasn't apt to go blabbing about something she was ashamed of, was she? But was it shame she felt? How much had she heard about the missing locket? Little pitchers . . . In the hall below them the others were drifting out of the living room and toward the dining room.

"Dinner's on." His mother called up to them, and Marny, looking relieved, ducked under his arm and flew down the stairs, two at a time. There was nothing he could do but follow her.

At dinner he found himself seated between Bibsy and the woman who was Cara's sister. Though he didn't look, he was intensely aware of Garfield Sumner across the table. He was determined to eat. To eat heartily. But even the soup made a lump in his stomach. And Bibsy was watching him. Nervously. With that "What-have-I-done" look. He'd have to talk with her. A straight talk. God knows he didn't want to hurt her. Why couldn't she see that he was changed beyond any repairing. "You Can't Go Home Again."

Across the table Garfield Sumner said to Lindsey: "Cara had an amethyst brooch, a gift from her father on her twenty-first birthday. She always said she wanted your Catherine to have it some day. She felt it looked like her. Whatever that means . . ."

"Bibsy," Johnny said, "let's clear out of here after supper. Let's go to a movie."

"But there's Cathy . . . And then this man, this detective. Your mother said he wants to talk to all of you. I'd thought maybe I'd better not stay after all . . ."

Everybody Adored Cara

"Nonsense," Cathy interrupted. "There's no reason why they can't go out, is there, Mommy? I'm sure anything Johnny has to tell the detective man can be told in three minutes. Johnny hardly knew Cara."

"I think we'll have to wait and see what Mr. Ridley wants."

"What is this?" Johnny said. "A subpoena?" He spoke not to his mother but to Garfield Sumner, and there was a rough and angry edge to his voice. He saw his father stiffen, open his mouth as if to speak, heard his mother's anxious warning cough, but Sumner was looking at him, daring him, needling him with the hard bright knowledge in his eyes, and he was not going to back away. "Who is this Ridley guy and what does he want to know?" His hand had slipped automatically to his pocket, folded around the locket, remained there consoled by the feel of it against his palm. "What if I don't want to talk to him?"

"I'll thank you to keep a civil tongue in your head," his father said.

And I'll thank you, thought Johnny fiercely, to keep out of this. His hand in his pocket tightened over the locket. He imagined himself bringing it out, dangling it before their dumfounded eyes. "I found this little trinket in my car. You take it from there, Sumner. Tell them how it got there. I'd like to know myself!" It was, as daydreams go, a dilly!

"Johnny dear," his mother said, "will you pass me the salt."

———

Tom took his time over dinner. The inn's dining room was cozy, dim lights and the music piped in of a smaltzy nature. His waitress was pretty and friendly, and the menu she gave him provocative. He ordered the lamb au Pierre, whoever he might be, and a glass of Chablis, and when the waitress wasn't busy he talked to her. Her name was Marie, and her husband drove a truck clear to Florida and back every other week. And she liked Stoningham all right, but she liked New Jersey better because that was where she'd grown up and where all her friends were. But after all, like her mother said, you can find friends anywhere, but a good husband is a rare come by. She just wished he wasn't gone so much of the time. That was why she'd taken this job. To keep from going crazy. She didn't look much over seventeen, and he felt somehow sorry for her. His tip was adequate but not lavish. He'd found that the more they gave of themselves the less they wanted in return. It was, he supposed, a matter of pride.

It wasn't quite eight when he left the dining room. He didn't want to get to the Merrills' too early. It wasn't far. He decided to walk. He hoped Sumner and his sister-in-law would have gone by the time he got there. If not he hoped Sumner would have the grace to leave. He didn't want him breathing down his neck.

Sumner was there. He made the introductions. "My partner Frank Merrill, Mrs. Merrill, Catherine, Marny, John, my sister-in-law Mrs. Gould . . . she leaves tomorrow, so if you have anything you'd like to ask her . . ."

"I would appreciate it then if *she* will stay"; Tom hoped his emphasis on the "she" would get the message across to Sumner, and it did. He made his "good nights" and then, hooking his arm through Tom's as though they were the best of friends and in complete accord, he propelled him into the hall. The moment they were out of sight of the others he dropped his arm and in a voice so low that Tom had to lean forward to hear, he said, "Watch the boy. Listen to the boy. Listen carefully to the boy." And without waiting for Tom's reply, he strode down the hall and out.

When he returned to the living room they were all, except Frank Merrill and his son, seated in a nervous semicircle around the coffee table. Merrill was making quite a business of filling his pipe from a canister on the bookcase, and the son hovered around the chair of a small, dark-haired young woman who for some reason had not been included in the introductions.

"Coffee, Mr. Ridley?" Mrs. Merrill said as though she'd been rehearsing the line for a play.

"Thank you very much." He didn't like to sit while the other men stood, so he remained standing in front of the coffee table balancing cup and saucer in the palm of his hand.

"I understand," Mrs. Merrill said, "that you will want to talk with us separately, and I think the television room is a good spot." Tom liked the way she had with the coffeepot, the cream pitcher, the sugar bowl; pretty hands and a deft way of using them. "Perhaps you have your own ideas about who comes first, but if you haven't, Johnny here . . . and oh yes, Bibsy, I don't believe you met her, Bibsy Michael, she is just here for the night, a friend of Cathy's, nothing to do with any of this . . . they would like to go out, so if you could take Johnny first . . ."

"I'd be glad to. Actually sequence doesn't matter a bit. So if you've any preferences . . ."

"Actually," the voice that broke in was familiar. The all-out girl voice on the telephone when he'd first called. She was sitting on the arm of a chair, legs crossed, a tall coltish lass with an affected hairdo and overdone eyes. The one he guessed called Cathy. "Actually Marny should probably come next after Johnny. After all, she should be in bed *now*. But if after that I could get it over with. I've got to go to work tomorrow, and I've a million things to do."

"Here, here, let's give Mr. Ridley some say so," her father chided. She flushed, and her glance which had rested on Tom with shy appraisal slid to the floor.

"You live in New York, they tell me," Mrs. Gould said. "A wonderful city, New York. Especially if you're a single man," she added on a note of inquiry.

"Wouldn't give you a plugged nickel for it," Frank Merrill said, "married or single. And what they're doing to it now shouldn't happen to Hoboken."

"That's the architect speaking," Mrs. Merrill smiled. Tom liked her smile. Candid. "Actually we've had some marvelous times in New York before we were married, while Frank was in school."

"It's a city for lovers," the child Marny spoke up, and at everyone's startled expression said, "at least that's what Cara says . . . said . . ." Tom looked at her. Brown hair, eyes, skin—some day when that button nose grew a little and the mouth . . . some day she was going to be a beauty.

"It's a city for everybody," he said to her. "Have you ever been there?"

"Once. At Christmastime. That's when I guessed about Santa Claus. That there wasn't any. All those toys in the windows. If there were a Santa Claus they would have been at the North Pole getting packed up."

It was good, this getting the feel of the people and they of him, but he could sense the boy's impatience, his boredom. He put down his cup.

"The television room you said?"

Mrs. Merrill nodded, and Johnny said, "I'll show you."

"Please," Mrs. Merrill intervened, "can't Marny be first? She's about to fall in her tracks."

"Sure, sure," Johnny turned back.

Marny, darting ahead of Tom, said, "Just follow me," and giggled. "It's silly, isn't it? Like playing post office. All of them waiting in there while we go out of the room."

"When did you ever play post office?" Tom trailed her across the hall and into a small, messy, lived-in room where he sat down on a leather chair beside a small table.

"Never," Marny said, "but I used to watch through the banisters when Cathy had a party. She hated it. Post office I mean. But it's what everybody wanted to play." She squirmed down into an armchair opposite him. "Is

Everybody Adored Cara

this going to be like when Chief Jones talked to me?"

"I don't know. What did he talk to you about?"

"About Cara going out and was I sure it was Cara."

"No. I just want to talk about Cara. Or rather I want you to talk about her. You see I never knew her. What was she like?"

"Nice."

"You liked her then."

"I still do." For a moment Marny's eyes filled.

"What did you talk about, you and Cara?" he said quickly.

"Animals mostly. We had a 'maginary cat. You see, Mother won't let me have a cat because of the birds, and she couldn't have one because of Garfield. His name was Chicory. We talked about him a lot, the things he did. He was a great big black Tom with white paws like boots. Sometimes we didn't talk about anything. Sometimes we just sat and thought."

"At her house?"

"In her vegetable garden mostly. She liked vegetables better than flowers."

"What else did she like?"

"She liked dressing up. She dressed up every afternoon even if she wasn't going anywhere. And she liked to cook. She taught me how to make brownies. Oh, and she liked to . . ." She stopped in mid-sentence and squeezed her hands together in her lap, not looking at him. "I guess I won't talk about that. I don't think she'd want me to."

"Did she ask you not to?"

"Goodness no. It isn't anything, really. I just don't think she'd like me telling everyone."

"Sort of a secret between you?"

Marny shook her head. "I don't think she even knew I knew. It's just sometimes I'd come unexpected . . . she said I had Indian feet, very quiet . . ."

"Was she cross with you when you came unexpected?"

"No. Mostly she'd just laugh and tease me about my Indian feet. Do you have any children, Mr. Ridley?"

"I don't even have a wife. Do you think Cara minded not having any children?"

"I never asked her."

"But she liked you."

Marny shrugged. "She liked all of us." She yawned sleepily. It was time to call it quits. At least for the present.

"You can run along now. Will you send your brother in?"

"It *is* just like post office, isn't it?"

"I wouldn't know. Like you I've never played the game myself."

The boy Johnny had given every indication that he would not be an easy subject, and the set of his jaw, the hard straight look in his eyes as he slouched into the chair just vacated by Marny was further evidence. Was it, Tom wondered, just his age, nineteen, twenty, twenty-one, the nature of the beast or, as Sumner had suggested, did he perhaps "know" something?

"Cigarette?" Johnny held out a newly opened pack, as though it were Tom who needed putting at ease.

"Thank you." He had his own cigarettes, but if it would make the boy feel better . . .

"Light?" He accepted that too.

"OK." Johnny said, leaning back. "Shoot! It'll be too late for even the late show if we don't push this thing. Mrs. Sumner was a friend of my mother's. I saw her coming and going every so often. But that's all I know about her . . . she was a friend of my mother's. If you had a mother you know how that is. Good morning, Johnny; Good evening, Johnny; and How is school, Johnny?"

The imitation was so apt, so reminiscent of his own

childhood that he grinned in spite of himself. "Yes, I know how it is. I gather it wasn't that way with Marny though. She calls her Cara."

"I wouldn't know anything about that." He flicked a nonexistent ash from the end of his cigarette.

"So far," Tom said smoothly, "everyone I've talked to has known Mrs. Sumner rather well. Perhaps you can give me a more detached picture. For instance, if you had to identify her for someone, how would you do it?"

"Small, blond hair, well dressed."

"You never noticed that she limped?"

"I guess so. It wasn't very noticeable." Another nonexistent ash was tapped into the tray.

"Would you call her pretty? Attractive?"

"Yes." He uncrossed his legs.

"Which?"

"Both." He recrossed his legs.

"Not beautiful then?"

The boy, seeming to consider this, had a harried look. "How the hell should I know?" he finally said. "Beauty is in the eye of . . . why not ask her husband?" The struck nerve quivered, the boy twisted in his chair. "What are you trying to get at, anyway? What's all this around the bush talk got to do with who killed Ca . . . Mrs. Sumner? Ask me something direct for a change. Like who do I think killed her. Ask me that."

"Who do you think killed her?"

"The guy who's paying you to find out. None other. That's what I think. *Think,* mind you. I don't know anything." He got to his feet. "Why didn't you ask me that half an hour ago and saved us both time!"

"Because," Tom said, "half an hour ago I don't think you would have told me."

Tom would have given his right arm for a short recess, preferably accompanied by a short brandy, but the girl

Cathy was in the door almost before Johnny was out of it. Detached from the myriad of strange faces that had confronted him in the living room, Cathy now appeared older than he'd guessed. She bypassed the more comfortable chairs and chose instead an armless straight back facing the window. She was wearing a tailored white linen which she tucked firmly about her crossed knees. Her sidewise glance was evasive, and she seemed not to know what to do with her hands.

"I saw you today," she said. "At Stone's. You were having coffee."

"The department store?"

"Yes. That's where I work. I was having lunch, Bibsy and I. I sat next you."

"I must have been very preoccupied not to have . . ."

"You were. The waitress . . ." She smiled, shifting her gaze to the darkness glazed window. "I thought her very pretty too."

"The hand that feeds . . ." he said. "I'm sorry I didn't see you. It would have been nice to find a familiar face waiting when I got here."

"I suppose it is awkward for you too, isn't it? I hadn't thought of that." She brought her gaze back to him. "I'd only thought of how awkward it is for me, for us."

"I'm sure it must be. I'll try to make it as, as . . ."

"Brief?"

"No. Un-awkward."

"Maybe if I could just start with what I think happened so you'll know, at least, where I stand."

"Start anywhere you like."

"Well, I think . . ." She leaned forward clasping her hands together in her lap. Pretty hands, competent too, and at the moment eloquent in their earnestness. "I think it was an absolute freak. Someone who broke in looking for something to steal. Cara was terribly careless about doors . . . anyhow, someone broke in, found her upstairs asleep, only she began to wake up and he panicked and then when he saw what he'd done he simply ran away without taking anything except maybe the locket because that was as far as he'd got when she woke up. It's the only thing that adds. May I have a cigarette? I don't really smoke so I don't carry them."

He gave her a cigarette, a light. "Why do you think that is the only answer?"

"Anything else would be out of character."

He grinned. "You mean she just wasn't that sort of person?"

"Maybe it sounds silly, but that's exactly what I mean."

"What sort of person was she?"

"Very kind and understanding. She liked people, and they liked her. That's what I really mean."

"She had lots of friends then?"

"Oh, yes."

"And liked to go out, take part in things?"

"I'm sure she did. Mother can tell you better . . ."

"Then you'd say she was happy?"

"Who is? All the time, that is."

"But generally speaking?"

"I don't really know. She had every reason to be."

"You are scowling. What is it?"

"I'm not sure I want to say."

"I see."

"Oh dear, now you'll think I'm concealing something dire. It's just that I'd never thought about it much, and besides it means talking about myself too, and well, I hardly know you." She flushed.

"I see," he said again.

On a quick intake of breath she said, "But you don't at all." And then, "I'm sorry. After all, Cara's the point. Cara and was she happy . . . Frankly I never felt I knew her awfully well, but I felt close to her somehow, and I think it was when I was unhappy or muddled about something that I felt the closest, as though she understood how

I was feeling, as though she knew just what it was like. Not from remembering, but from knowing."

"And how were you feeling at those times? I'm not being personal. Again the point is Cara."

"Unsure, as though all the wonderful, splendid things were going on somewhere else and you'd never find them or they you unless you hurried ... I used to call it growing pains until I realized Cara felt just the same way a lot of the time, and then I guessed maybe it was just the way I was and that we were somehow alike."

"And you never talked to her about this?"

"Not actually. It was sort of an antenna thing."

"And you only picked it up when you were depressed?"

"Restless is a better word, but I can't see where all this soul-searching is getting and frankly I feel as though I'm being disloyal. If Cara was unhappy she wouldn't want anyone to know it."

"I can understand how you feel, but all this is important. Very important. Please bear with me a little longer."

Again she flushed and veered her glance away. She really was awfully young and vulnerable.

"What sort of things did you and Mrs. Sumner talk about?"

"Anything, everything." She smiled. "Actually I guess I did most of the talking. Cara was what is known as a good listener ... books, music, politics, religion, dates or the lack of them ... she did a lot for my self-confidence."

"In what way?"

"This isn't fair!" she exclaimed almost harshly. "You'll know everything there is to know about me, while I ..." She broke off and, looking at him with an expression that could only be described as cornered, said, "She told me that one day I would be a very beautiful woman."

"And so you shall," he said gently, and added because gentleness wasn't really enough, "What would you like to know about *me*, Miss Merrill? That I too hanker for the places where all the wonderful, splendid things are happening without me? That even at twenty-seven I occasionally find myself riding a white steed through the woods around Nottingham Palace or getting to my feet to receive the acclaim of a packed courtroom for my unrivaled brilliance in solving an unprecedentedly complicated crime; that, in short, growing pains are not limited to the very young."

"I'm not the very young," Cathy said. "I'm almost eighteen. But thank you, thank you very much." Her smile was radiant.

"Now is there anything else about Mrs. Sumner . . ."

"Not that I can think of now. Later if I . . ."

"What about Mr. Sumner? You've known him a long time, haven't you?"

"Practically all my life."

"Like him?"

"I guess so. I certainly don't *dis*like him. As a matter of fact I had sort of a crush on him when I was about ten. He is handsome, you know, and so terribly correct. It was my matinee-idol stage. But he never paid the slightest attention to me, not even fatherly attention."

"You must have known his first wife then."

"Yes, I did. Helen. Only I always called her Mrs. Sumner. Even after she told me to call her Helen."

"Any special reason?"

"She looked like Mrs. Sumner, acted like Mrs. Sumner, was Mrs. Sumner. Not Helen. You know how kids are . . ."

"Do you remember much about the divorce?"

"Nothing. It was kept very hush hush. I didn't know a thing until one night Garfield came to dinner alone, and then Mother told me. I remember that I was shocked. I'd always thought of them as sort of the epitome of a couple, handsome, dignified. They seemed to fit. Not that I think there was much love, and of course that's proven now, but they just seemed right in a proper, formal way. Mother told me it was simply a matter of incompatibility, which shocked me even more. I still haven't figured it out. If they didn't have anything else, they had that."

"Were your parents upset about it?"

"Daddy was. He has an absolute thing about divorce. And it always upsets him when someone he thinks he knows well does something unpredictable. But I don't think Mother minded too much. She never really liked Helen. They had nothing in common, and Helen made quite a lot of being the senior partner's wife. Position meant everything to her. But why are we talking about her? She doesn't even live in Stoningham any more."

"Background." He eased himself out of the chair and stood up. "Well, I guess that about covers it. You may not know it, but you've been a big help."

"I don't see how. I really haven't told you anything. Just a lot of prattle."

"Prattle is simply undisseminated fact. Yours to prattle, mine to disseminate." He grinned. But even with the grin he was afraid it came off on the pompous side. And he found he didn't want her to think him pompous. He found he wanted her to go on looking at him in that half-shy, half-eager way as though she thought he was very, very special. "Nobody's infallible," he blurted. "I only hope to God I can bring this case off."

"I do too," she said. "Not just for Cara and all of us, but for you."

Johnny and Bibsy didn't go to a movie. There was nothing Johnny wanted to see. Nothing, that is, light and airy and emotionally undemanding. They went instead to a nightclub on the outskirts of town that had an orchestra and didn't mind selling liquor to minors. He knew that Bibsy's mother would drop dead if she knew, and that even Bibsy wasn't too happy about the deal, but ever since the conversation with Ridley he'd felt reckless. It had been a reckless conversation when you came right

Everybody Adored Cara

down to it, and he could kick himself all over the lot and back. Ridley was no fool. And he knew he hadn't heard the end of it. Not by a long shot.

Bibsy, with her head ducked a little, as though she wished to be incognito, headed for a corner booth. Her and her prissy timidities. Why couldn't she just once forget the "watchbird." Do what she wanted to do with bravado. Be herself.

"What in hell *is* yourself, Bibsy?" He slid into the booth opposite her.

"Please, Johnny, can't we just relax tonight? Enjoy being . . ." "Together" he supposed was what she'd been going to say. "I'll even have a drink if it'll make you feel better."

"That's just what I mean," Johnny said. "If you want a drink, have one. If you don't, don't. Not for me or anybody. For yourself. Waitress!"

The place was fairly crowded for a Monday, and it was awhile before she got to them. In the interim he could see that Bibsy was wrestling with whether or not and all at once despised himself for bullying her. "Look, Bibs, don't mind me. I'm in a nasty mood tonight."

"I know." The eyes tilted upward, at least the lids, the frame, so that when she looked down the effect was definitely Oriental. "So why did you ask me to go out with you?"

"Impulse. I wanted to go somewhere . . ."

"And not alone."

"And not alone."

"The play going badly?"

"Yeah." The waitress was beaming down upon them.

"One scotch and soda," he said and looked at Bibsy.

"Make it two . . . Well, at least," she said when the waitress had gone, "you've got the temperament to be a writer."

"It takes a lot more than temperament." He leaned

back, glad to be on safe ground again. Safe and sane ground. "The only trouble with writing is that you never really know what you're doing. Not from one day to the next. And when you think you do, look out!"

The young man couldn't be much older than Johnny, Lindsey thought, facing him across the television room, and he looked tired.

She said, "I hope my children haven't been giving you a bad time." It was just something to say. She was surprised at his reaction.

"Only your son," he said. "Johnny doesn't seem to want to talk." He didn't smile when he said it, and for the briefest moment this angered her.

"It was only that he was in a hurry. He had a date with Bibsy. Patience is not his strong point."

"I see," Ridley said, but she didn't believe him.

"Also he's very emotional," she enlarged. "He knew Cara less well than any of us, and yet I feel that this has upset him enormously. More than any of us realized. He keeps his emotions under wraps. He probably didn't want to talk because he was afraid of showing them."

"He showed them."

"I mean his *true* emotions." She was beginning to feel that possibly the young man was not as young as he appeared and, for some reason, it made her uncomfortable. Like not knowing exactly who was on the other end of a telephone.

"He showed those too. He thinks Mr. Sumner killed his wife. At least that is what he said."

"You're making this up." But he didn't look like the sort of young man who made things up, and she felt all at once as though the floor were sliding out from under her. She felt it was a very good thing that she happened to be sitting down. "Did he say what he based this preposterous assumption on?"

"He said he didn't *know* anything, but this was what he thought."

"Perhaps he was just trying to be funny and thought of course you'd know it. He has a terribly wry sense of humor sometimes. And if he was angry . . ."

"He was angry."

"Then that explains it," Lindsey sighed and rested her head against the chair back. "I'm sorry he was rude. He's rather at sixes and sevens this summer. He's writing a play. Or trying to. And giving us all rather a bad time. I hope you won't feel you have to report this to anyone. It really was inexcusable whatever stupid nonsense he meant by it. I shall have a talk with him."

"I'd rather you wouldn't," Ridley said.

"But he must be made to see . . ."

"I'd rather you'd leave that to me." The young man's manner was pleasant enough, but still she felt it not so much a request as an order, and she didn't like taking orders from strangers. Certainly not where her children were concerned.

"I'm afraid that is out of the question," she said crisply, and at his look of rebuked small boy, repented the crispness. His wasn't an easy task . . . "May we talk about Cara now? Perhaps there I can be of some real help. I was awfully fond of her and want to know, need to know, what happened. Haphazard as her death may prove, everything, even unpremeditated murder, must have some underlying pattern."

"I'm glad you feel that way," the young man said, his dignity restored. "So few people understand what I'm trying to do, and it's so simple really . . . looking for the pattern. They think only the murderer really knows what it is or why, but the victim plays a part in it, the second lead, and the victim is all you ever really have to work with . . . Tell me, what was Mrs. Sumner like?"

"I'll do my best," Lindsey said, "but it won't be easy.

She was a most complicated woman. I think, or else so simple . . . Not that it mattered. You couldn't help liking her . . ."

It wasn't until they started home that Johnny realized he was not simply high, but looped. The road didn't stay where it was supposed to be, and the headlights of the cars coming toward them danced giddily up and down. "I think," he said to Bibsy thickly, "that you'd better drive." He brought the car to a wavering halt at the side of the road.

"But I don't have a license," Bibsy said. "I've only driven a car about three times in my life. That was something I was going to do this summer . . ."

"It's only your neck I'm thinking about. I don't give a damn what happens to mine."

"If you put it that way." She moved over as Johnny clambered out of the driver's seat and made his bumbling way around the car. "Oh, why did you have to have that last drink? Anyone could see, could tell . . ." She turned a button that sent the windshield wiper into a frenzy of pointless activity. Tried another and leaped out onto the road, jerking Johnny forward against the windshield.

"Maybe this wasn't the answer," he said.

"The drinking?"

"No, your driving."

"Why, Johnny? Why the guzzling? Getting blotto isn't going to do the play any good."

"To hell with the play!"

"That's just what I mean . . ."

"Look, Bibsy, look Bibsy, old girl, let's knock off the lecture. Leave this little moment of anesthesia be, this little moment of, of, un-reckoning, this time out of context. Look, Bibsy, leave *me* be. Me!"

"I've a good mind to do just that," she said, removing her foot from the gas for one thoughtful moment. "Leave you and your old car right here by the side of the road. It won't be the first time I've had to walk home."

"Not with me. Not with me you haven't."

"And he wasn't half as drunk or as mean as you are."

"What was he then?" He turned to peer at her uncertainly in the light from the dashboard.

"Brash. And conceited."

"Poor Bibsy. He probably liked you."

"Poor him then."

"No, poor Bibsy," he sighed deeply and slumped to the window.

"We're home," Bibsy said presently. "You simply can't pass out now."

When she got no response she ran her fingers over his face to see if his eyes were closed. They were. He stirred and fumbling for her hand, held it to his face, and she felt his tears spilling against her palm, running down her wrist. With a little moan she drew his head to her shoulder.

"Cara," he murmured. "My beloved, Cara," he said, and was silent except for his breathing, which was heavy and slow. The breathing, she realized, of one who, drunken, sleeps.

She sat rigid and cold, bearing the weight of his head and remembering as though it was being said to her here and now the words of a psychology teacher spoken many months ago. "Youth," he had said, "absorbs shock and heartbreak as easily as a baby absorbs its bottle . . ." It isn't true, she thought, and began to tremble. Gently, firmly she moved the limp head from her shoulder and slid toward the car door. As she opened the door Johnny slumped sideways into the place where she had been, arms about his head. One of the arms looked cramped. She rearranged it.

There were a few scattered lights burning downstairs in the Merrills' house. She hoped they were lights that had been left on for herself and Johnny and that there was no one still up and about. Her plan, if anything so hazily and tremulously evolved could be called a plan, was to slip unseen and unheard up to Cathy's room and into bed.

She hadn't thought of the possibility of the front door being locked, but it was, and the key undoubtedly buried somewhere in Johnny's pocket. She stood weighing the worse of two alternatives, to knock or to search the unconscious Johnny's pockets. It took only a moment to decide. She returned to the car, and after trying vainly to rouse him, set about the unaccustomed and distasteful business of going through a man's coat pockets.

If the key weren't in the coat pockets she'd have to give up. Trouser pockets were another matter entirely, and besides, from an engineering standpoint, virtually impossible. However, her first foray brought out a key and something else twined about it, a chain . . . it was too dark to see exactly what, too dark to untangle here. On the lighted front porch she had no difficulty. The chain turned out to be a delicate gold affair with a gold heart, a locket, attached to it. Something shimmered and beat at the back of her mind, but never quite congealed. She supposed she should return the necklace at once to Johnny's pocket, but she was sick with hovering over that insensate form and as weary with love as if she'd spent the night in his arms. She put key to lock and it was, thank God, the right key. The necklace she slipped into her pocketbook.

The house was blessedly still. As she tiptoed past Mr. and Mrs. Merrill's room on the second floor she heard voices within, but no light shone through the cracks around the door.

Cathy's room was around a corner and to the left. Cathy's door was open, the light beside the bed was on, and Cathy sat cross-legged on one of the beds painting her toenails.

"I thought you'd never get home," Cathy said.

"You shouldn't have waited up."

"I had to. I've so much to talk about. Oh Bibsy, it *was* him, one and the *same* . . . and he treated me as though, well, he acted as though . . ."

"Is this the detective fellow?" Bibsy sank down onto the spare bed and kicked off her shoes, began unbuttoning her dress.

"Of course. Why do you *always* have to take the edge off things? Doesn't it mean anything to you that I'm in love?"

"I'm sorry. I didn't realize . . ."

Bibsy gave her a forlornly regretful glance which must have revealed far more than she intended, for Cathy said, "What's happened? You look like the end of the world. Where's Johnny? I didn't hear him come up, did I?"

"No. He's out in the car sleeping it off."

"You mean he's passed out? Johnny?"

"Solid. Cold."

"But he's never done this before!"

"That you know of . . ."

"That damnable play! I'm beginning to feel just as rabid on the subject as Dad." Having waved her feet in the air to dry the polish she now jumped off the bed and reached for her robe. "Why didn't you tell me right off? We've simply got to get him in the house . . . to bed . . . if Dad ever finds him there . . ."

"We can't carry him"—Bibsy went deliberately on with her undressing—"and he won't be roused. Don't think I didn't try!"

"Maybe some cold water on his face and coffee . . ."

"It'll just make a lot of bustle and confusion, and your parents are still awake. I heard them talking when I came by their door. Leave him alone. He'll come out of it before morning, and no one the wiser."

"Do you really think so?"

"I'm sure of it," Bibsy said with all the certainty of one who knows from long and arduous experience.

"Then this has happened before?" Reluctantly Cathy

shed her robe, got back on the bed, sat, knees hunched under her chin disconsolately.

"Not with Johnny," Bibsy said and added because there no longer seemed any reason not to. "My father." She was already in bed, and now she turned on her side, her back to Cathy, and closed her eyes.

"I didn't know," Cathy said. "I guess there's a lot I don't know. I'm sorry, Bibs."

"Don't be."

"I mean that I've been so, so, unaware."

"I wanted it that way. I still do."

Cathy was quiet for so long that Bibsy thought she was asleep; hoped she was. Her chest burned with the weight of unshed tears. But presently Cathy said, "Did you and Johnny have a fight?"

"Nothing that personal."

"How did he act?"

"Like he'd had too much to drink."

"Silly, I mean before that?"

"Oh, Cathy, that was so long ago . . . Can't we go to sleep?"

"I'll try. I wonder if he's asleep . . ."

"Of course. It'll be hours before . . ."

"I don't mean Johnny."

He wasn't asleep. He was lying on his back in his bed at the Stoningham Inn trying to figure out what it was between Garfield Sumner and the Merrill boy.

In the dark of their room Lindsey and Frank Merrill lay talking in hushed voices.

"I can't see what this Ridley fellow is getting at," Frank said. "And I don't like having the children dragged in. Keeps them all churned up. Cathy looked as though she had a fever when she went to bed."

"Marny's eating it up."

"I don't like that either. And what can she contribute, when you come right down to it?"

"She did see Cara go out that night. A rather pertinent point..."

"But did she? She's got plenty of imagination and a hound dog's nose for publicity."

"I think she probably did. The way she told me, matter-of-factly, as though she had no idea it was important."

"But where would Cara go by herself at night?"

"Really, Frank, you make it sound so sinister! A hundred places—for a walk, to the mailbox..."

"The fact is, wherever she went, if she did, she came home to be murdered. I'd call that fairly sinister."

"I still think they're going to find it was a freak, a break-in, a..."

"I hope you're right."

"You sound dubious..."

"Of course that's the *easiest* thing to think, a coincidence, a happenstance..."

"Then think it. Please. I simply can't face anything else." It was on the tip of her tongue to blurt out about Johnny and Ridley ... it would be such relief. If only she could count on Frank to see it as she had and not get angry with the boy ... too much to expect ... she herself was angry with him ... really angry ... such a stupid irresponsible thing to say.

"Guess I let that super sleuth upset me tonight. He asked the damnedest questions!"

"He's got a theory that if he can ever really get to know Cara, *really* know her inside and out, he'll know, not who exactly, but the sort of who that might want to kill her."

"It wasn't the questions that bothered me. It was realizing how little I did know her *or* Garfield for that matter." He turned toward her then and drew her to him. "It made me wonder if maybe I'm just dumb about people or if..."

"Yes?" It was a whisper.

"Or if this is going to turn out to be a very nasty business all around."

Bibsy woke with the first jangle of Cathy's alarm. She hurried into her clothes and gathering up her pocketbook was at the door by the time Cathy, stretching reluctantly, opened her eyes.

"Be right back," she explained hastily. Though there were sounds of life upstairs and down, she encountered no one. The latch had been sprung on again on the front door . . . a good sign. She sprinted across the dew-wet grass to the driveway where Johnny's car was parked under a maple tree. There was, as she'd hoped, no Johnny. She took the locket out of her pocketbook and placed it on the seat of the car where it would appear to have fallen from his pocket. This plan had occurred to her in her last waking moments the night before; had, in fact, made it possible to sleep at all. The idea of returning it to him in person, her explanations, and worse, his, should he feel compelled to make any, had weighed heavily on her. This way he need never know and she, she would just try and forget it. It was possibly a trinket belonging to one of his sisters, or something he meant to give them. The other thing, the tears, his tears, and the spoken name, she could not forget. Nor did she wish to. For all the first fresh sharpness of pain, her heart's slower wisdom told her that however she might be suffering she now understood much that had hurt and baffled her. She felt in a strange and almost comforting way closer to Johnny than ever before. It didn't occur to her that his grief sprang from any more profound a source than unrequited love.

Johnny slept late. The first real dreamless sleep he'd had in nights. So it wasn't Johnny who found the locket on the seat of his car. It was his father. Frank, discovering a flat tire on his own car, went in thundering search of a

Everybody Adored Cara

wrench Johnny had borrowed from him weeks earlier.

When he saw the necklace he thought it belonged probably to the Michael girl who'd been out with Johnny the night before. It was a pretty little thing and must, he thought, amused and reminded of his own courting days, have dropped off in the scuffle. Something rang a faint bell as he examined the piece and eventually he realized why. It somewhat resembled Garfield's description of the missing locket. What heart-shaped locket wouldn't? Had he found it in any other place he might have thought he'd really found something. The wrench turned up under the seat.

He took the necklace into the house and because Bibsy and Cathy had already gone to work, he left it on the hall table, calling to Lindsey as he did so, "Tell Johnny I found his girl's chain. It's here on the hall table." And then because he'd already kissed Lindsey goodbye once, and because it was late and he still had a tire to change, he went out.

Lindsey, with Marny's help, finished the breakfast dishes. She had meant to give Garfield the cards from the flowers the night before, but in the confusion of the detective's arrival and Garfield's almost immediate departure, she'd forgotten. She got them now, out of her desk, and was almost out the side door when she heard someone knocking at the front. She went back through the kitchen and into the hall where she saw that it was Garfield himself, and smiling, waved the cards at him.

"Mental telepathy," she said as he opened the unlocked screen door and came in. "I gather these are what you've come for."

"If they're the cards, yes. How did you know?" He started toward her and abruptly, as though he were riveted there, stopped beside the little hall table with the mirror behind it. She thought for a moment he must have caught a look at himself in the mirror and been shocked by what he saw, but her eyes following his glance, saw that it rested not on the mirror but on the table itself and that a curious smile played about the corners of his mouth. Almost before she'd realized what it was he saw, he'd scooped the neck piece up in his hand and held it dangling between them.

"Cara's missing locket," he said quietly. "Have you any idea how it got here?"

"Why no, why yes. I mean I think you must be mistaken. That belongs to Bibsy, Bibsy Michael, the young girl who was here last night, Cathy's friend."

Marny, sidling through for a return visit to the kitchen, eyed the locket anxiously. "It's not Bibsy's," she said. "It belongs to Johnny."

And then because, having known trouble herself she wanted to be sure she did the right thing by Bibsy, she said, "Of course maybe he gave it to her."

"I still think," Lindsey said weakly, "there's some mistake." She wished that Garfield would go and let her straighten this thing out in her own way, but he obviously had no such intention.

"Here," he thrust the locket into Lindsey's unwilling hand, "take it into the light. I think you'll find a small, almost infinitesimal scratch on the lobe of the gold heart and that one of the links in the chain is mashed up near the clasp . . ."

Almost defiantly she walked to the door, held it up to the bright June sunlight. Even so, she had to look closely. Garfield couldn't possibly have ascertained these minute defects in the shadowed hall. The little gold heart spun giddily in the light and her own heart felt as though it too were spinning.

"Marny," she said, and her voice seemed to spin, to spiral in her ears, "why do you say this belongs to Johnny?"

"Because it does, because I know it does . . ." Marny for some reason looked close to tears.

"How do you know?" Lindsey pursued mercilessly.

Everybody Adored Cara   115

She didn't look at Garfield. She couldn't. Why didn't he go! Take the damnable trinket and go!

"Have I got to tell?" Marny was looking from her to Garfield as though she too would find all this easier without his presence.

"Yes, you've got to."

And so she told, about the candy, about the locket, about being caught, about Johnny's anger, growing redder and smaller with shame with every word until at the end Lindsey went and caught her up in her arms.

"There, there, my love. It could happen to anyone," she murmured and buried her face in the soft brown hair as much for her own comfort as for Marny's.

"I'm not angry with you, Marny," Garfield said.

"Nor with anyone yet I hope," Lindsey said, putting Marny down. "Until we know more . . ." she said, holding out her hand to give him the locket. "Until we know more I'd be grateful for your silence."

Their eyes met and he, albeit reluctantly, seemed about to concede when they heard someone catapulting down the stairs behind them and turned to find Johnny, bare chested, clad only in jeans, hair uncombed, standing at the foot of the stairs, looking at them blankly. Slowly his eyes cleared, the blankness gave place to a bright hardness that brought Lindsey's heart thumping up into her throat.

"Excuse the garb." He spoke directly to her, ignoring Garfield, "But I hardly expected guests at this hour. Has Bibsy gone yet?"

"She's gone"—Garfield took a step toward him and opened his hand to show him what he held there—"but if this is what you're worried about . . ." There was triumph in his every gesture and naked hatred in his eyes.

"Don't!" Lindsey cried. "Let me handle this!" She moved between them, but Johnny ever so gently pushed her aside.

"Where did you find it?"

"Here on your hall table," Garfield said smoothly, "and now I'd like to know how it got there?"

"That I can't tell you," Johnny said, angrily.

"But you admit knowing this was Cara's locket?" His measured anger cut through the boy's fury like lightning through a cloud.

Lindsey turned to shoo Marny away, out . . . but for once Marny didn't need to be told. She was already gone. Frightened no doubt by their voices and the ugliness of what they said.

"You know damned well I knew. And why!"

"Johnny!" Lindsey grasped him by the arms, shook him. "Stop and explain! At once!"

The shaking, her voice, seemed to bring him to his senses. He looked down at her, the brightness, the hardness fading a little from his eyes. "Stay out of this, Ma. Go for a walk. To the store . . . wherever it is you go in the morning . . ."

"Stay out of *what?* What were you doing with her locket, Johnny? I, Garfield, we've a right to know. And calmly, reasonably . . ."

"Okay. I found it in my car the night after Cara died."

"And said nothing to anyone?" Lindsey's voice broke. "How could you be so stupid? Didn't you realize . . ."

"Of course he realized," Garfield interrupted coldly, "that's the point. However he got hold of it he realized. I'm sorry to do this to you, Lindsey, and to Frank, but I'm afraid there's much you don't know about your son. He said nothing to anyone because he was in this thing up to his ears. Right, Johnny?"

"Will you get out of here?" Johnny said, his hand balling into a fist. "Will you?"

"Perhaps for now it would be best," Lindsey touched Garfield's sleeve pleadingly. "Perhaps when we've all cooled a bit . . ."

"I'm sorry, Lindsey," Garfield said and walked briskly toward the door.

"You won't say anything, will you? Not for a while?" Lindsey called after him helplessly.

"Let him!" Johnny bellowed. "Let him tell the world!"

"Tell the world what?" At the door Garfield turned. "Tell them what, Johnny?"

"That I gave it to her! That I loved her!" Johnny's voice rang out. Half-crouched, he held his hand flat against his side as a man sometimes does when he's about to spring.

Garfield flung the screen door open and slammed it shut behind his erectly retreating back.

Stricken, drained, Lindsey let herself down onto the bottom step of the stairs and began very softly to cry. She felt rather than saw Johnny come and stand nearby, felt rather than saw his belated anguish.

"Is it true, Johnny?"

"Yes, it's true."

"Young men often become infatuated with older women. It doesn't mean . . ."

"This was no infatuation," Johnny said flatly.

Lindsey raised her head and looked at him.

"The locket? Did you . . ."

"Yes. I gave it to her. Garfield must have found out. I don't know how because she never wore it. I never saw it again after I gave it to her until the other night."

"The night that . . . ?" Panic choked her.

"No, no. The *next* night. In my car. On the seat of my car. Just the way I said."

"But how did it get there?" She clasped her hands together hard in her lap and looked at him beseechingly.

"I think she put it there—that she wanted to return it," Johnny said. "And I don't want to talk about it any more."

Tom Ridley was up early writing down the things he'd been too tired to write down the night before.

Marny Merrill, about eight, imaginative, candid. Relationship with the deceased . . . they shared an imaginary cat and a certain pleasure in long contemplative silences. Have the impression the child put more into the friendship than the woman.

Johnny Merrill, nineteen or twenty, twenty-one, sensitive face without being the least effeminate. Handsome but so far unaware of the fact or not caring. Moody. Hostile. Toward me? Or Sumner? Or both? Feelings toward Mrs. S. far more intense than he admits to. Yet almost entire family claim he knew her least of any of them. Including Johnny!

Cathy Merrill . . .

He leaned back and looked at the name smiling. But when he started to write his impressions beneath it, he found he didn't want to. He didn't want to commit that glowing, shy girl-woman to the professional jottings in a notebook. Not because he minded, but because he knew that she would. And he didn't want to do anything that she would mind his doing. Even if she would never know he'd done it. Or not done it.

The dining room of the inn was virtually empty at this early hour, and he had the waitress Marie to himself. She brought him a paper and then didn't let him read it. She was in fine spirits. Her husband was due in that night. Two days earlier than she'd expected him. It meant he wasn't bringing much of a load which meant not much commission, but it wasn't the money that counted with her. It was the companionship. Sure she saw a lot of people on her job, talked to a lot of people, but she didn't feel like she got to know anybody. And this wasn't much of a town for finding things to do.

"Pretty dull town, Stoningham," he agreed, and then

flipping thumb and forefinger at the day's story on the murder . . . a headline saying *NOTHING NEW ON BLUE CHIFFON* and below it four paragraphs of rehash . . . he said, "But you do have your small excitements. Been following this?"

She put a plate of bacon and eggs before him and looked over his shoulder. "Nothing new, hmm. And I doubt if there'll ever be. Just one of those things. Some hood kid looking for loot and panicked. The first Mrs. Sumner was staying here at the time. She thought the same."

"She was here?"

"Yeah, she always stays here when she comes back. Not that I knew who she was at the time. Not until they sent a man around from the paper to ask her what she thought about what had happened. He cornered her right at this table while I was getting up her dinner, so I heard parts of it. Ready for a second coffee?"

"What did she think about it?"

"Like I said . . . some hood kid. But she didn't want to talk about it, and I don't blame her. Like she said it was all water under the bridge, and what she thought at this time was no one's business but her own. Polite as you please, but froze that reporter clean out of the place. A real lady!" she sighed in admiration and refilled his coffee cup.

"Did she seem upset at all?"

"Who wouldn't be? It could have been herself. It's a shame that other one had to wake up. She'd be alive today most probably if she'd just slept through or pretended to."

Frank Merrill was dictating a letter when Garfield, without announcing himself or knocking, burst into his office. He knew something had happened and guessed with some excitement that it probably had to do with the case. Garfield's curt dismissal of the secretary without a by your leave from him, corroborated this. It seemed to take Miss Timmons minutes to gather up pad, pencil, and the Kleenex box that was never far from her reach, and in those minutes, Garfield paced the floor impatiently, but when finally she had gone, closing the door behind her, he appeared not to know what to say. He sat down in the chair still warm from Miss Timmons' tidy posterior, but in a moment was up again and walking.

"I wanted to see you first," he said finally, speaking rapidly now that speech had come to him. "First. Before I see Link Jones. I felt it only fair to let you know what I was doing. What I've got to do." Suddenly he was beside the desk and reaching into his pocket pulled out the chain and locket that Frank had found earlier in his son's car and tossed it onto the desk in front of him. "Cara's missing locket," he said. "Johnny had it. He's had it for some time. By his own admission he was in love with my wife."

Frank had felt like this once before in his life. Once outside a dive in New York a sailor had punched him in the stomach. Square in the stomach. It had sent him reeling to the sidewalk. He was surprised now to find he was still sitting upright. But his stomach felt like that. The same.

"Why you Goddamned lying son-of-a-bitch," he said. And it was just what he'd said to the sailor all those many years ago.

But Garfield, instead of coming at him as he half-expected him to, as he half-hoped he would, said, "I only wanted to prepare you. And it's just as well I did. I doubt if the police would be as understanding of your reaction." He scooped the chain up in his hand and pocketed it.

"I'm sorry," Frank said above the angry roaring in his ears and got up and went to the window because he didn't want to look at Garfield or let Garfield look at him. He heard the door open and close. He turned then and lifted the telephone receiver off its hook, but he didn't lift it to his ear, nor did he dial a number, and in a moment he let it fall back into place and sant down at his desk and buried his head in his arms.

On second thought Garfield didn't go directly to the police. He went first to the office of Rufus Lewis, his lawyer. Rufus was having coffee, and he sent out for another cup for Garfield. "Well," Garfield said, "I've got Cara's locket, and I've got her murderer!" But somehow the declaration didn't come out on the triumphant note he'd expected it to. Rufus looked at him blandly as though this were a joke and he was waiting for the punch line. When no punch line was forthcoming, his eyes widened, and he said, "You mean Ridley has cracked the case already?"

"Not Ridley. Me. It's Frank Merrill's boy Johnny . . ." He held up a protesting hand as Lewis seemed about to interrupt him. "You find it hard to believe because you don't know the whole story. It's not a pretty one. I hoped I'd never have to tell it to anyone. But if justice is to be served . . . and I'm determined it shall be . . . The fact is the boy was in love with my wife. He has just admitted it. I've known it a long time . . ."

"And your wife?" It was the lawyer's voice, crisp, hard, brooking no evasions.

"My wife encouraged him," Garfield said. They were the hardest words he'd ever spoken, and afterward he sat very still waiting to feel something. Shame. Regret. The old bitter anguish. But he felt nothing.

"How do you know this?"

"I made a point of finding out. After Cara refused to tell me where she'd got the locket I began checking on her —her whereabouts, the mileage on the car . . . Her account of how she'd spent the day often failed to jibe with the mileage on the car. Too often for coincidence. And always it was a matter of twenty to twenty-three unexplained miles. One day I pulled the old trick, said I was going out of town and didn't go. Put my car in the garage for a check-up, got them to lend me another and parked about a block from the house. Around three she came out and got in her car. I followed her at a distance, sometimes letting a car come between us. I followed her as far as the abandoned store where you turn off to go to the Merrills' lake cottage. She turned in beside the store and stopped. I looked at my speedometer. It had been eleven miles exactly. I drove on up the road, turned my car off the highway and waited. I thought then it was going to be Frank who came to meet her. I couldn't believe it, but there didn't seem to be anything else to believe. But it wasn't Frank, it was Johnny. When I saw Cara get out of her car and into his and drive off toward the lake, I should have followed them. Had it out then and there. That's what I should have done. But how often does a man do what he should, Rufus? I hadn't thought past finding out who she was meeting, and I couldn't think past it then.

"I turned around and went home, and when she came in looking fresh and innocent as a child, I asked her where she'd been. She said she'd meant to drive out to Gaine's farm for some fresh strawberries but that unfortunately her car had conked out on her and that if young Johnny Merrill hadn't happened along and picked her up, she'd probably be there now." He stopped and swiped at his sweating forehead with a handkerchief.

"And you believed her?"

"Of course not. But I pretended to. What else could I do? I'd muffed my chance. I had to wait for another one."

"You say you found the locket?"

"Johnny had it. He's admitted to having it ever since the night after Cara died. Said he found it on the seat of his car."

"Did he give any reason for not mentioning it before?"

"Half a dozen."

"Have you been to the police?"

"I wanted to talk to you first. I wanted to ask you how much of this I'm going to have to tell them."

Rufus, watching him, thought there was nothing quite so painful to witness as a man of dignity and reserve stripped of all privacy. He'd seen it often, of course, here in his office and in the courtroom, but he'd never got used to it.

"All of it," Rufus said.

After breakfast Tom called the Merrill house. He wanted to talk to young Johnny Merrill again and to the little sister. Mrs. Merrill answered the telephone. She sounded as though she either had a cold or had been crying. Gone was her graciousness of the night before. She was curt almost to the point of rudeness. She said that neither she nor her children were or would be available for any further questioning. He hung up feeling stung and baffled. He looked ruefully down at his list of appointments for the day . . . a Mrs. Carmichael who had worked with Cara Sumner on the May Day committee . . . Dr. Whitney (he had been most pleasant on the phone but said there was little he could contribute as Mrs. Sumner had been a remarkably healthy woman, and he could count on one hand the number of times he'd seen her) . . . an operator at the beauty parlor Mrs. Sumner frequented . . . and somewhat more promising, the Sumners' maid . . . But with the Merrill family closed to him, it was going to be hard going.

With an angry expletive he crumpled the list in his fist, and just as he did so the telephone rang. It was Garfield Sumner. He had called to tell him that he would no longer need his services. He himself, he said triumphantly, had solved the case. The murderer, as he had suspected all along, was the Merrills' son, Johnny. He asked Tom to send a bill for his services to date. He didn't wait for Tom to ask any questions. He hung up.

Tom waited until he could open his mouth without swearing, and then he called Rufus Lewis. It was Lewis after all who had hired him. It would have to be Lewis who fired him.

"I've just had a call from Mr. Sumner," he said without preamble. "He tells me the case is solved. Anything in it?"

"No case is solved until the jury is finished with it," the lawyer said, but there was enough that was placating in his voice to tell Tom what he wanted to know.

"Then you think . . . not that it matters." He broke off and laughed shortly. "I've been fired."

"I'm sorry he put it that way."

"I never quite got the feeling we were on the same side." Tom drummed a pencil against the desk top. "'And now that I think about it maybe we weren't. Young Merrill, he said. What's he basing it on?"

"The locket. Johnny Merrill had the locket. He has also admitted to an affair with Cara Sumner."

"That *kid?* Is that enough evidence to accuse him of killing her?"

"To hold him as a material witness, yes."

"From where I sit, and that is neither here nor there, it looks like Sumner had more of a motive . . ."

"Sumner was in Chicago at the Blackstone Hotel," Lewis said flatly.

"Well, it was fun trying. And you can tell Sumner there'll be no bill."

"I'm sorry as hell about all this." Lewis sounded as though he meant it, and on this meager note of comfort Tom hung up. He went and sat on the side of the bed and stared out of the window on umbrella tops and a few midmorning coffee drinkers gathered beneath them. No wonder Mrs. Merrill had cut him off earlier. Thinking about them, the Merrills, the girl Cathy, he could be almost glad he was out of it. Almost . . .

Everybody Adored Cara 125

Johnny didn't close the door of his room. It was only a matter of time before somebody would come. His father, Link Jones . . . and he didn't want to sit behind a closed door waiting for a knock. Deliberately, methodically, because he had nothing better to do, he showered, shaved, and put on a shirt and slacks. He switched on his record player, not bothering to see what was on the turntable. It turned out to be *Tales of Hoffman*. The light, giddy music suited him fine. He lighted a cigarette and sat down in the open window and shut his eyes, and letting the music wash through him, thought of people dancing, long-ago people, in elegant, inhibiting clothes . . . He and Cara had danced together at the lake once . . . a waltz, because that was all she knew or wanted to know. "I can only lend myself to the waltz," she'd said and flushed . . . He never knew whether it was because of her lameness or some other shyness. Fortunately years ago as a small boy forced to attend dancing classes once a week, he had learned to waltz.

Downstairs a door banged shut, and his father called to his mother. He must have been listening for it or he'd not have heard above the music. He turned the record player up and looked at his watch. It was almost noon. He went back and sat in the window, but now when he closed his eyes there were no dancing people. Only darkness. He thought, I should go downstairs. Get it over with. But he neither opened his eyes nor moved. Presently the music ended. He got up and turned it off. Voices drifted up the stairwell, but he could barely distinguish one from another. He put on the *Hoffman* again and waited. He waited almost an hour before he heard his father climbing the stairs. His steps were slow, and when finally he stood in the door, Johnny thought, So this is how he will look when he's old . . .

His father closed the door behind him. "Sit down, son," he said, and himself sat on the straight chair, turning it away from the desk so that it faced into the room. Johnny returned to the window sill. For a moment his father let his gaze wander around the room as though he'd never been inside it before and found it confusing. There was much Johnny wanted to say. Too much. There was no place to begin. So he said nothing while his father got his bearings, while his father made up his mind where to begin. He began with the locket.

"Did you give the locket to Cara?"

"Yes, I told Mother . . ."

"Why?"

"Because I loved her."

"And she?"

"She . . ." He hesitated, wondering if still there might not be some way of protecting her. "She accepted it."

"Did she, er, ah, return your feelings?"

"Look, Dad, I'm sorry about what this has done, is doing to you and Mother. And I don't expect you to understand. But I won't, I can't talk about it."

"Don't you realize that you are going to be forced to? And not only to us?" His father had never sounded, never been, more patient. This alarmed him more than what his father was saying.

"I realize Garfield is trying to pin Cara's death on me. But he can't." Good God, his father didn't think . . . but apparently he did . . .

"Where were you that night, Johnny?"

"Right here. In my room. Writing."

"We heard you go downstairs, your mother and I. At about midnight."

"To the kitchen, for food . . . Christ, Dad!"

"I'm only trying to give you some idea, some inkling of the sort of questions you are going to be asked."

"For a minute there I thought . . ."

"And rightly," his father interrupted, "that too." He sighed and took a deep breath. "Look, son, I don't give a damn what you tell anyone else, but your mother and I must have the truth. Whatever it is. We can do nothing

Everybody Adored Cara   127

to help you without it. And we want to help you. With everything we've got and in every way we can."

Stunned, wounded beyond speech, Johnny stood up and walked the length of the room. It was a small room. It didn't take long. Not long enough. His own parents, and they knew him no better than that! Let them stew then. Stew in their doubt. Their . . . He stood over his father, looked down at him, the angry words on the tip of his tongue. Then his father looked up, and there was nothing in his father's eyes but pain. Only that. And there'd been nothing in his voice but love. Only that. He put his hand on his father's shoulder and grinned shakily.

"I may be all kinds of a damned fool, but I'm not a murderer. I didn't kill her. Why would I?"

"Because she threatened to tell Garfield? To have no more to do with you?"

"Is that what that son-of-a-bitch is saying?"

"Sooner or later somebody is going to say it. I thought it better be me." His father was looking at him hard now. Without pain, without love, just hard and clear.

"There were never any threats between us. I loved her. I don't know who killed her unless Garfield did. Does that answer you?"

"It answers *me*," his father said and stood up. "I've called Sam Watkins, my lawyer. He's going to be here any minute now. He'll go to the sheriff's office with us."

"The sheriff's office?" Just like that! "What for? What can they . . . ?"

"They can hold you as a material witness. They've got enough evidence for that. And that is what they plan to do."

"Lock me up?" There was no panic in that. Just wonder. Johnny Merrill behind bars. A guy that had never deliberately hurt anyone in all his life! But undeliberately? There you had something. However crazy this show got, he must remember that. It would seem that un-deliberately Johnny Merrill had hurt a lot of people He must remember that for whatever it was worth.

"I very much doubt that," his father was saying "There'll be a hearing, and then I presume they'll set bail And now if I were you I'd put on a less spectacula shirt and a tie." At the door his father hesitated. "There i one thing I must say in all fairness to Garfield. And to you. He is absolutely and sincerely convinced that yor killed his wife."

Johnny bit back his retort. As long as his father wanted to believe this, he'd not argue the point. It was something he could do for him. Not much but something.

Tom Ridley, throwing his meager necessities into his briefcase, thought wryly of the last time he'd taken leave of this town. That too had been in a sense under fire. That other time had been a far more grievous one, but the emotions were somewhat the same, the minor ones a least. The hurt pride, the feeling of unfinished business, o failure. But what the hell, he hadn't failed this time! He simply hadn't been allowed time enough. And yet, and yet, given time, all the time in the world, would he have come up with Johnny Merrill? He sat down on the bed to consider this. In all honesty. "The truth now, Ridley," he scowled. "Well, maybe not Johnny," he scowled, "but the affair, the affair with another man. I might have come up with that. Eventually. Once I got Cara together, al together in one piece. The truth now . . . Well, maybe might never have got her together . . . God knows the picture is, is . . ." He got up and pulled his notebook ou of the packed briefcase and once more read over every thing he'd been able to find out about Cara Sumner. And he knew then what the trouble was, what the trouble had been. There was plenty of information here. But, as Gar field Sumner had said, "everybody adored Cara." His note read like the saccharine revelations of a fan magazine

Everybody adored Cara. But somewhere in this mean, hard, old world there must be someone who hadn't. Someone who could have given him the other side of the coin. Revealed some telling weakness. A note of dissonance.

His post-mortem was interrupted by the ringing of the room phone. The voice, though glutted with emotion, he recognized at once. It was Cathy, and she was either very hurt or very angry or both.

"I'm sure you're very proud of yourself, Mr. Ridley. But you're wrong this time. You and your 'method'! If you had any perception or feeling at all, you'd know after talking to Johnny for five minutes that he couldn't kill a flea! Oh, oh, oh, how could you . . ." The voice cracked into a despairing whisper.

"But I didn't!" Tom all but shouted. "I didn't have a damned thing to do with . . . Where are you now?"

"At Stone's. It's my lunch hour . . . or rather half hour. . ."

"If I come right over now? . . . I would like to see you before I go . . ."

"Before you *go?*" And then before he could absorb the misery in her voice, "Oh, of course, naturally, now that the case is solved, quote, unquote, now that 'Detective Snap Judgment' has finished his wretched business . . ."

"I'll meet you at the lunch counter at Stone's in five minutes," Tom interrupted, and before she could protest, hung up.

He wasn't at all sure she'd be there, but she was. Clinging to a chocolate soda and not quite looking at him. She opened her mouth to speak, but he headed her off.

"I'm going to do the talking," he said. "And when I've finished you can say anything you want, but not until . . . First, it was Garfield Sumner who put the finger on your brother. I didn't know anything about it until he called me up and fired me. Now, I'm not saying that if I'd suspected, thought even, that your brother was involved, I'd have hesitated to say so. I'm not saying that. But I didn't suspect it . . ."

"You mean you didn't, you don't think that Johnny . . ."

"I didn't. I don't know what I think now . . . I haven't had time to evaluate the evidence."

"But you've had time to evaluate Johnny."

He was about to protest this, but she was looking at him with such trusting confidence that he couldn't. "What are you wanting me to say, Cathy? That I think your brother is innocent? Is that what it takes to make us friends again?"

"Not if you don't think it."

"I told you I don't know what I think. And what difference does that make now anyway? Isn't it enough that I didn't have anything to do with what's happened? That I'm glad I didn't?"

"Of course it does." She smiled ruefully. "I'm sorry I was so . . . but you see I liked you and, and absolutely trusted you, and I couldn't bear to think . . ."

"That I'd accuse your brother?"

"Without telling me or any of us a thing about it . . . it seemed sneaky and too . . ." She looked at her watch and gasped. "Heavens, I've got to run."

"And too, what?"

"And too, it would have been a mistake, a terrible mistake, because Johnny didn't do it. I didn't think you were the sort of man who made mistakes, not terrible ones. I was disappointed." She put her soda money down on the counter, and he picked it up and gave it back to her.

"So as next time you have a soda you'll think of me."

"Then you *are* leaving?" She was off the stool, poised for flight.

"What else?"

"A lot else . . . Well, better luck next time . . . for both of us," she said, and left him to watch her walk

Everybody Adored Cara

swiftly away, the upsey, flouncy hairdo teetering with every step.

A lot else, she'd said. Sure, sure, stick around and solve the case. On his own time. With no cooperation from anybody any more. And nothing to go on but a girl's faith in him and a boy's probable but by no means proven innocence. The staggering illogic of women! He paid for her soda plus tip and walked slowly, thoughtfully, back to the inn. When he got there he went to the desk and told the clerk he wasn't signing out after all. Not that day. Maybe tomorrow.

He then asked for a look at the registry. Helen Stone Sumner's signature wasn't hard to find. She had a large firm hand that ran to curls and dashes. She gave as her address Route 1, Hastings, a town, the clerk informed him, was some seventy-five miles away, a two-hour drive at the most. Maybe Helen Sumner and Cara Sumner had never met, but he would bet his bottom dollar that at least here was someone who did not adore Cara. It wasn't much of a lead, but it was something to do until he could think of something better. A talk with Johnny Merrill, for instance, if his sister could arrange it.

He didn't dare telephone the ex-Mrs. Sumner in advance and risk a conclusive No. He'd just have to take his chances on finding her at home. It was a dull hot seventy-five miles, and at several points he asked himself what the hell he was doing here when he colud be halfway to New York, the whole wretched business behind him. But finally he was on the outskirts of Hastings, a little two-by-four village, and finally he was in the drugstore asking how to get to the Sumner place on Route 1. The druggist, an opulent and, judging from the absence of customers, a lonely man, went into detail. Two blocks down and on his right there would be a yellow house; turn right there and on down a hill and out past Hart's filling station, and from there the quickest way across to Route 1 was right, but straight ahead was a better road and prettier, only he'd best not miss the sign a quarter of a mile past Hilltop Dairy . . . Tom interrupted to say he thought he'd prefer the shorter route and got out pencil and paper.

". . . a white house with green shutters on the left of the bridge." Tom had no difficulty finding it. Surrounded by untended fields, it stood in a copse of trees, a curiously city-bred little house for so informal a setting. High narrow windows all shuttered as though whoever lived here did not really like the country if the truth were known. A paved driveway furthered the notion. There was, he was happy to see, a car parked on it, at the side of the house, near the rear. A black coupe with whitewall tires. He had no sooner turned off his motor than roaring out of nowhere came a German shepherd. He stood beside the car door and bared his teeth in no uncertain fashion, barking and growling intermittently, pausing only long enough to glance now and then toward the house as if he looked there for approval of the performance. Tom tried speaking to the animal, but this only sent him into further frenzies and presently, to Tom's immense relief, the front door opened and a woman came out onto the stoop and called to the dog. He went to her at once and sat beside her, ears cocked, waiting further developments. Tom got out of the car and walked across the tidily clipped lawn toward them. They made a formidable pair, the woman and the dog. She was tall and thin and had once, it was easy to see, been handsome. It was in her bearing and the bone structure of her face, a face now too drawn and harsh to be called anything but old.

"I'm Tom Ridley," he said, when he was close enough to speak.

"Yes?" The dog bristled, and she put a restraining hand through his collar.

"I'm looking for a Mrs. Helen Sumner . . ."

"Yes?"

"I'm a detective working on the Sumner case. I wonder if I might have a word with you." He tried to make his smile reassuring.

"Your credentials?"

All that he ever carried was his detective's license. He showed this to her. She studied it a moment.

"You see, I've been so bothered by reporters . . ." she explained, returning it to him, and with a weary shrug that could have meant anything, she led the way into the house.

The interior, like the exterior, seemed more designed for the city than for the country. The parlor, or was it a library, which she took him into, was small and dim and elegant. She indicated an upright, velvet-covered, straight chair and would not be seated until he seemed about to seat himself. A small thing but one that made him exceedingly uncomfortable. And he couldn't help wondering if that hadn't been her purpose. Or was it simply nerves on her part? For once settled she couldn't seem to remain there but hopped up to find him first a cigarette which he didn't want and then to attend to something in the kitchen. When she returned she started talking at once.

"I did so hope the wretched business would be solved by now. After all, Stoningham isn't so large that . . . I can't imagine what I can contribute. As you undoubtedly know I've had no contact with Garfield since the divorce, but anything I can do I shall be more than willing to . . . I bear him no ill will. I'm not one to nurse grudges or harbor resentments. He has my deepest sympathy."

These statements were scarcely concomitant with the harsh austerity of her face, but it wasn't her feelings toward her ex-husband that had brought him here.

"I'm sure he has," he said glibly, "and you can be of enormous help. You see, so little is known of the late Mrs. Sumner prior to her marriage. Unpleasant as it may be for you to think of these things now, I was hoping you might be able to throw some light . . ."

"Then you hope in vain," she said, interrupting him. "I

never knew of her existence until I read of my hus . . . of Garfield's marriage in the paper!"

He'd struck a nerve here, and he prodded it. "Then they'd not met at the time of the divorce?"

"I didn't say that. I said only that I knew nothing of it. Of course, it is obvious that they must have. They were married days after the decree became final. And Garfield is not an impetuous man." She breathed deeply and sighed. "But that is all over, past . . ." Abruptly she was again out of her chair. "I'm cooking a roast," she said by way of explanation and hurried from the room. When she came back her face seemed to have softened, and her manner was light, pleasant, almost teasing. "If you've come to hear anything unpleasant about Cara"—she settled herself in her chair comfortably, as though she meant at last to remain there a while—"you've come to the wrong place. Though I never knew her, I never heard anything unkind said of her. I gather she made Garfield very happy indeed."

"Then the divorce was your wish?"

"Of course not. But what earthly bearing has that?"

"It makes you a most remarkable woman, Mrs. Sumner. That you should have no bitterness toward a woman who . . ."

"See here, young man! What right have you to poke and pry in this manner? I've told you all that I know of Cara. And now I must ask you to leave." When she stood up she used her hands to help her, and he noticed for the first time that for all their long-fingered look of breeding, they were very powerful hands indeed. "You've not been honest with me. You have some ulterior motive in coming here. What is it?" The hands now that they'd done their duty by her had begun, he saw, to tremble.

"I swear to you," he said, troubled to have upset her, "I only wanted a new, a perhaps not so biased perspective on the late Mrs. Sumner. Frankly I wanted for a change to talk with someone who had no reason to be fond of her."

"The roast!" she exclaimed in an agonized voice and fled. He had no idea if she intended ever to return. Shaking his head in puzzlement he found his way to the front door. Opened it.

"Aren't you even going to say 'goodbye?'" Her voice floated out to him from the dimness of the hall and in a moment she appeared, swaying ever so slightly, her face as serene as a newly spread coverlet. He knew, of course, even before he caught the faint odor of wine that drifted from her throat when she spoke, what the roast must have been all about. "I'm sorry I couldn't have been more help." She held out the long-fingered hand but did not use its strength on his, rather let it lie in his palm helplessly for a second and then removed it. "But you see I'm so out of touch with things here."

"I'm sorry if I upset you," Tom murmured.

"Heavens, lad, no one upsets me." From the doorway she called to the dog who had taken a stance beside Tom's car. Reluctantly the dog came, casting a sidelong glance at Tom as he brushed past him through the door.

Tom didn't look back, but he had the feeling that she and the dog remained in the doorway looking after him until he and his car were out of sight.

Bibsy's lunch hour that day had been changed so that she didn't run into Cathy until closing time when she went into the employees' lounge to patch up her face and tidy her hair for the bus trip home. Cathy was sitting cross-legged on one of the sofas smoking, but the moment she saw Bibsy she untangled herself and leaped up as though she had been waiting for her.

"I'm not riding the bus home," she said at once. "I simply can't face all those people. I'm going to take a taxi. But I thought I should tell you or you might have waited for me."

"I probably would have," Bibsy said laconically. "Wherefore this sudden aversion to the common herd? You used to like rubbing elbows . . ."

"Then you haven't *heard*? It's in all the afternoon papers. Everyone in my department is talking about it and looking at me as though . . . I thought I'd at least be able to make it home before . . . oh, Bibsy, it's Johnny." The room was filling with chattering salesgirls, and she dropped her voice so that it was almost a whisper. "Garfield Sumner has accused Johnny. They're holding him for questioning. I'll call you later, but I've simply got to get out of here . . . all these gaping hyenas!"

Before Bibsy could get her breath, Cathy was gone. Bibsy looked about dazedly trying to remember what it was she was doing here. Slowly she went over to one of the mirrors and taking a comb out of her bag, jabbed at her hair. Next she got out lipstick, but in the mirror she noticed that the hand holding it was trembling uncontrollably, so she put it back in her bag. The newsstand at her bus stop blazed out at her: *PARTNER'S SON HELD IN BLUE CHIFFON MURDER*. Just to make sure she leaned down and looked until she found Johnny's name. John Bladen Merrill. So that's what the B stood for. She'd always wondered, but whenever she'd asked him, he gave her a teasing answer, "Backward" or "Barewolf" and once "Bedeviled." "Johnny Bedeviled Merrill, that's me." She didn't buy a paper. She didn't want one. The bus came. She got on it, put her money in the box, and then quickly before the doors could close, she got off it. A bus would bring home upon her too quickly. Home and her mother waiting with the paper spread across her knees. Walking would take longer. And the overnight bag she'd taken to the Merrills (Could it have been only last night?) didn't weigh much. But it was over a mile, and she was tired from her day's work. When she came to a little park she chose a bench in the shadows and sat down. It was a mistake. She began,

Everybody Adored Cara

the moment she wasn't doing anything, going anywhere, to cry. I must think, she told herself. But all that came of it was her sobbing and the conviction that they couldn't do this to him, that they mustn't, that somehow they must be stopped.

Presently her crying stopped and she found to her astonishment that she didn't feel nearly so tired. It was getting quite dark. She got up and began again to walk toward home, but the walking seemed easier, and her thoughts easier, more coherent. By the time she reached her house she was almost ready to face her mother. Her mother and the whole world. The whole cockeyed world that could call Johnny Merrill a murderer. What she planned to do seemed so simple, so logical, that it amazed her that no one had thought of doing it before. Cathy or Mrs. Merrill or someone, anyone who loved him. And trusted him.

Her mother was not in the living room as she'd expected her to be, she was on the telephone, and when she heard Bibsy come in turned an anxious face and said into the telephone; "Here she is now. Sorry to have bothered you."

Putting down the receiver she said to Bibsy, "Why didn't you call when you found you were going to be late? You know how I worry . . ." Bibsy walked down the hall toward the kitchen, her mother following . . . "Tonight especially . . . when I thought that only last night you spent the night under the same roof with that . . ."

"Don't say it, Mother!" Bibsy stopped and squared around. "Don't say anything you'll be sorry for!"

"Me sorry?" Her mother's eyes filled. "It's you that should be. Sorry because you wouldn't listen, wouldn't heed, when all I wanted, all I ever wanted was to protect you. I knew you were over your head from the start with those Merrills, but you wouldn't listen. I didn't want you hurt, that's all." Her mother reached a tentative hand toward Bibsy's shoulder, but Bibsy backed away.

"I know, Mother. But we all have to live our own lives. Make our own hurts. What would you like for supper? Is there any of that stew left?"

"I don't want any supper. I had a sandwich with my tea." It was the voice of reproach.

"In that case," Bibsy said. "I shan't bother to eat either. Bed is what I really want the most." She yawned elaborately and moved toward the stairs.

"You *have* seen the paper tonight, haven't you?" Her mother was looking all at once uncertain and perplexed.

"Yes, Mother, I've seen it. But there's not a word of truth in it. There can't be because, you see, I was with Johnny that night, all of that night until five o'clock in the morning."

"What are you saying!"

"That I'm in love with Johnny Merrill. That I sneaked out and met him that night. That it was not the first time . . . that he couldn't possibly have . . ."

"Impossible! You were asleep in your bed. You couldn't. You wouldn't!" Her mother began to cry. "Why do you torture me in this way?"

"I'm sorry, Mother."

"You're making it up!" her mother cried. "That's what you're doing. Making it up to protect him with never a care about what you're doing to me!"

She had expected this. Was prepared for it. "I loathe what I'm doing to you," she said softly, "but it has to be done." This new firmness, this new strength that she had begun to feel taking root in her like some tentative seed must have made itself known to her mother, for she seemed at last to believe her. Her mother's crying had stopped, but she was very pale and her mouth worked in an agony of wordless shock. Finally in a strangled voice her mother said "Have you told anyone? Anyone besides me?"

"Not yet. But of course I shall have to." She leaned

against the newel post for support, bracing herself to meet protest.

"Please!" Her mother moved toward her, hands outstretched. "Please, please, daughter. Don't! I, your father . . . everything we've tried to do for you, wanted for you. And you, what will become of you? You know what they'll say? What they'll think? . . ." Her mother interrupted herself to stare at her daughter with fresh disbelief. "It wouldn't be true, would it, Elizabeth? What they'd think?"

"Of course not. It's just that Johnny and I wanted to talk to . . . well, you've always kept such tight strings on me, made it so hard with that eleven o'clock curfew . . ."

"I *had* to. Don't you understand that with people like us we have to be extra careful if we want to be somebody and not just trash . . . oh, Elizabeth, don't you *see?* You *can't* tell them." The beseeching hands reached and clutched hers. "The Merrill boy will be all right without you crucifying yourself. If he's done no wrong he'll be all right. They'll see to that . . . They have the money, the influence. Everything. While we have only what you're thinking of throwing away . . . our standing . . . our good standing. Why just today Mrs. Flowers was saying how lucky we were in our daughter. Such a lady, she said, so . . ."

"It's no use, Mother. I know what I've got to do. I've made up my mind. I can't unmake it now. If I unmade it now I'd never feel good about myself again."

Her mother let go her hands and with what sounded more like a whimper than a moan, turned and made her thin bent way into the living room. It was the helplessness of that aging back that was almost Bibsy's undoing. What, she asked herself suddenly, bitterly, has Johnny ever given me that I should take so much away from her? But this was no reasoning matter, a thing to be weighed with the mind while the heart pounded out its own unreasoning answers. She wheeled and flew up the stairs to her room before love and compassion would overwhelm her.

Cathy didn't know what she expected to find at home . . . her mother prostrate, her father in a rage, Johnny already gone, carted off to some never-never land devised for people "under suspicion of murder" . . . nothing would have surprised her, and the nearer home she got the more fervently she wished she'd ignored her mother's command over the telephone that morning to stay put and had bolted her job and gone to them. At least by now she would have been a part of whatever awaited her and not quivering with apprehension.

As she passed the Sumner house she deliberately averted her eyes and realized that already she'd begun to hate Garfield Sumner. She'd never hated anyone before in her life that she could remember and the sensation, the physical sensation, was not a pleasant one. She hurried on to her own walkway. There was a strange car in front of the house, but it was not a police car as she'd half-expected it might be.

The house seemed quiet enough. The door to the television room was closed and no one was in the living room. The only sounds came from the kitchen. There she found her mother, her arms covered with flour, making, of all things, a cake.

"Where's Tina?" Cathy said.

"I gave her the afternoon off." Her mother looked up. Her eyes were red-rimmed and her nose had a red splotch at the end of it. "I didn't want anyone extraneous around . . . besides, I wanted something to do. Here, will you beat this a bit while I start the icing?"

Gratefully Cathy took the beater. "Who belongs to the car outside?"

"Sam Watkins. He and your father and Johnny are in the TV room. I couldn't stick it."

"Sam Watkins?"

"The lawyer."

"Well, at least Johnny's here. I wasn't sure, I didn't know..."

"Poor lambie. I should have told you. It's not that bad. So far. We posted bond."

"Maybe you'd better brief me. That is, if you don't mind talking about it. All I know is that Johnny had the locket and Garfield accused him . . . just what you told me. I didn't want to read the papers. Is there anything more?"

"A little," her mother said and looked at her curiously, shyly almost, and then taking a deep breath said, "It seems that Johnny was very much in love with Cara."

"But she was old enough . . . puppy love!" Cathy tossed her head. "What has that got to do with anything?"

"Nothing if Cara hadn't encouraged him. But unfortunately she did."

"Encouraged? What do you mean encouraged? Cara encouraged everyone. She encouraged me. She . . ."

"I mean something quite different," her mother said almost angrily.

"But they never even saw each other. And when they did Johnny was positively surly. I simply can't . . ." Cathy shook her head struggling with this new concept of her brother, of Cara, of love. "It does explain a lot," she said, as much to herself as anyone else. "Poor Johnny . . . is he in a terrible state?"

"He seems quite calm. I think actually he's relieved."

"He's not scared?"

"If he is he isn't showing it.

"Are you scared?"

"Not really. It's different for me, for a woman. We have kind of sublime faith in the verities, in all the things our menfolk tell us about truth and justice. Your father is badly scared." Suddenly her eyes filled but Cathy, not knowing what to do about it, pretended not to notice.

"Do you suppose Tom guessed?"

"Tom?" Clearly her mother scarcely remembered.

"Mr. Ridley, Garfield's detective," Cathy said tonelessly. Maybe give a few days or weeks or months she too would scarcely remember. She hoped that was how it would be.

"No, I don't think he did," her mother was saying, "but he would in time. He seemed to have a way of getting to the heart of things. He upset us all, I think. Even you. That last was more query than statement and Cathy, wrestling with whether to tell her mother the why of this, realized that had it been Cara she wouldn't have hesitated. But her mother was not Cara. Her mother would hear her out with patient amusement, and when she'd finished her mother would be very careful not to say anything that would let her know that she thought it all rather touching bit of foolishness.

"Well, anyway, that's over," she said aloud.

"Mr. Ridley? Yes, I suppose Garfield would feel there was no longer any point . . ."

"Whatever he thinks he fired him. How can Garfield be so sure about Johnny? How does he dare!" She felt her neck and face burning with this new emotion, this thing she'd felt for the first time in her life passing his house earlier. "You know what I think! I think Garfield found out about Johnny and came sneaking back from Chicago and . . ."

"No!" her mother interrupted harshly. "I won't have that kind of ugliness in this house! We must keep our hearts clean. We mustn't let this nightmare thing change us, use us . . ." The ringing of the telephone cut off whatever else she'd been about to say. There was an extension in the kitchen and her mother picked it up.

"Yes, she's here. Right here." Her mother's perplexed frown as she gave her the receiver told Cathy it wasn't Bibsy, and of course the moment she heard that voice she knew exactly who it was. Himself. No other.

"Then you haven't left yet?" She tried to keep her voice somewhere below high C, but she wasn't sure she succeeded.

"I'm just beginning to like the town. Can I see you? For dinner maybe? I've had a rather interesting afternoon. I'd like to tell you about it."

"Dinner?" She panicked, her free hand flying automatically to her hair which would have to be washed and what dress . . . "Just a minute." Cupping her hand over the receiver she said, "Mummy, may I go out to dinner with Tom Ridley? May I please?"

"You mean he's still . . . I thought he'd been dispensed with."

"He has . . . only not by me."

"But we don't know anything about him, and isn't he a good deal older?" Lindsey frowned, weighing wisdom against her daughter's radiant, upturned face.

"That's just it. I want to know more about him," Cathy pleaded. "Please."

Radiance won. Her mother nodded an uncertain approval.

"I'll pick you up about seven," Tom said.

Bibsy undressed quickly and got into bed, but sleep didn't come as soon as her exhaustion had led her to expect. She heard her father come in. Heard the low murmur of voices in the living room. Heard her parents mount the stairs. Outside her door one of the footsteps stopped, and in a moment her father's voice said, "Come, Muriel. Let the child sleep. We'll tackle her in the morning. Maybe she'll be more sensible for a good night's rest."

The steps moved away from her door, but the muffled duet of voices continued in the room across the hall for what seemed interminable hours. Maybe they were right. Maybe in the morning she would be more sensible. If you wanted to call it that. More frightened. More weakened by their misery. More herself, fastidious, cau tious, a quivering prey to the opinion of anyone an everyone. The Bibsy that she, and yes, Johnny, despised The one that had lost him.

All was quiet in the room across the hall now. And ha been for some time. Bibsy slipped out of bed. It was to warm for either robe or slippers. She took only the can dle on the table beside her bed. But she didn't light until she got to the kitchen and closed the door behin her. The telephone usually sat in the hall, but it had a lon extension wire, long enough to reach under the kitche door and to the kitchen table. Her mother had planned this way. She liked to sit at the kitchen table of a mornin drinking coffee and conversing with her friends. In th dark of the hall she'd not been able to find the telephon book, so she dialed information and asked for the residenc of Chief of Police Link Jones. He had a rough sleep voice, and he didn't sound as though he put much cre dence in what she was telling him. And he asked he some ugly questions. Such as who was paying her to d this. And did she know the penalty for perjury in th state. And was she willing to testify before a judge? He exhaustion lent authenticity to her replies. Or must have because Chief Jones seemed at the end to believe he She explained that she had to be at work at nine an arranged to meet him at his office at eight the nex morning.

This time when she lay down on her bed she was aslee the moment her head touched the pillow. And if sh dreamed or stirred she didn't know it.

The only other good restaurant besides the inn th Tom knew about in Stoningham was a small steak hou where he had used to take that other girl, so he left th decision of where they were to eat up to Cathy. Sh directed him to a place called Fargo's which turned ou to be the very small steak house where he'd spent so many ecstatic, so many wretched hours, but having conveniently forgotten its name he didn't know this until they were there and it was too late to make excuses.

However, it had been done over. A different color scheme, and in place of the juke box was a piano and a girl in evening dress that played it. He did have to head Cathy off from the corner table which had been "their" table, but after that the other girl began to fade.

They ordered dinner and a manhattan for him, sherry for her.

"I'd much rather have the manhattan," she said, "but I told Mother I'd 'behave discreetly.' Sherry *is* discreetly, isn't it?"

"In my mother's house it was called 'tonic' and whenever we got sickly or run-down we were forced to drink a glass of it before meals. I was almost a man before I found out it was anything more than that." He smiled. "You too have a wise mother. Did you tell her why I wanted to see you tonight?"

"Why no, I didn't know, I wasn't sure . . ." Her face fell. "Why *did* you decide to stay on?"

"To help if I could. I thought you'd know that."

"I did, I do . . . but I guess I also thought . . . never mind what I thought . . ."

"That it was because of you? Because you'd asked me to?" He tried to catch her eye, to make her smile with him, but she had eyes only for the little glass she twirled between her fingers on the table top.

"I didn't ask you to. I merely . . ."

"You merely, and then I merely, and now here we are. Aren't you even going to ask me what I did this afternoon?"

"What did you do this afternoon?" Suddenly she smiled and their eyes met, and her smile spilled into laughter. "I'm such a fool," she said, shaking her head at what a fool she thought she was.

"You are quite the most refreshing thing that has happened to me in a very long time," he said solemnly. "What I did this afternoon was to pay a call on the first Mrs. Sumner at her home."

"In Hastings? Would she see you?"

"I didn't give her a chance not to. I just arrived."

"But Tom she isn't, she doesn't . . . Whatever for?"

"I wanted to talk to just one person, just one, mind you, that had no reason to like Cara Sumner, had, in fact, every reason to hate her . . ."

"But she never knew her . . . never saw her . . ."

"You don't have to know or see a person whom you think has harmed you to hate them. One thing is certain and that is that Garfield divorced his wife to marry Cara and that he asked his wife for a divorce long before she was willing to give it to him. Now, accepting that premise, wouldn't you expect Helen Sumner to be just a trifle bitter?"

"Was she?"

"No. She had nothing but the most saccharine things to say about both her husband and Cara. But in order to say them she had to make several trips to the pantry for a shot of 'courage juice.' By the time I left she was almost reeling."

"Poor woman," Cathy murmured.

"That's just my point," Tom said. "She's suffering from a lot more than the death of her husband's second wife. And why did she lie to me about how she felt about Cara?"

"Pride maybe."

"Pride doesn't have to be laced with spirits to make it stick!" he scoffed. "No, Cathy, that's a scared woman. And specifically she was scared of me."

"You're talking in riddles," Cathy said. "And I haven't the slightest idea what you're driving at."

"I'm dealing in riddles," Tom said. "And I haven't the slightest idea what I'm driving at either. All I know is that Helen Sumner knows something . . . and I grant you it may not be at all important . . . but she knows something she's afraid will be found out. I'm not going to rest until I find out what that something is and neither is she."

"Did she know about Johnny?"

"I don't think so. But by tomorrow she'll know. And I'd like to see if it doesn't change her tune a bit."

"You don't really suspect her of murdering Cara, do you?" Cathy sounded let down, disappointed in him. "Frankly, I'm beginning to think it was Garfield whatever he says about Chicago . . . I think . . ."

"Garfield was in Chicago," Tom interrupted bluntly. "That has been thoroughly checked out. And no, I don't suspect Mrs. Helen Sumner of murder, but I do suspect her of withholding something. She was in Stoningham the night it happened, remember? Cut her visit short. And is now quietly going to pieces in Hastings with no one to know except a monster of a German shepherd dog. She is the first person I've talked to since I've been working on this confounded case that has given me one shred of hope of ever solving it. So please let me float my little bubble while it lasts. And if we don't eat this steak pretty soon it's going to get up and walk away!"

Johnny awoke from a boyhood dream of trout fishing to hot, slatternly sunlight and the sound of distant thunder. The telephone was ringing. It was probably that that had pulled him away from the cool mountain stream high in the Adirondacks where he and his father had used to vacation when he was little. The ringing stopped and in a moment his mother knocked on his door and came in.

"Link Jones is on the telephone. He wants to speak to you. He sounded, well, almost cheerful." His mother's eyes rested on him with the same look of pained perplexity they'd worn ever since yesterday morning. "At any rate I don't think it's anything to be alarmed about."

"I'm not alarmed," he said gruffly and gave her shoulder a reassuring pat on his way out.

"That you, Johnny?" Cheerful wasn't the word for it exactly, but the Chief certainly sounded less fierce than he had the day before.

"Speaking."

"Know a girl named Elizabeth Michael? Nickname of Bibsy?"

"Yes, sure. She's a friend of my sister's."

"She says she's a friend of *yours*."

"Well, any friend of my sister's is . . ." But this was no time for being smart. "Right," he said, and wondered if the Chief was going to try to tie in that last date with Bibsy with the locket or what . . .

"Have you ever dated her?"

"A couple of times. Maybe more. But as I say, she is mainly a friend of my sister's."

"She seems like a nice girl," Link mused. "Neat and particular."

"Very much so."

"Honest, dependable. Not a bit flighty like some."

"Right." Damned if he didn't sound as though he were about to hire her and wanted references.

"Shy? A girl who'd hate any kind of publicity?"

"You've got the picture." Impatiently Johnny shifted feet.

"In short, anything she'd say would be the truth and nothing else but?"

"I'd put my money on that any day."

"That's how I figured her. Well, looks like you're in luck. She came clean for you. And without you squealing. Like to see that kinda chiv'lry in kids. Don't come by it often."

"Look here, I haven't the damnedest idea what . . ."

"It's OK, boy. You don't have to cover up for her. She said you'd try to. But there's no need. We'll play it down. Real down. Just a couple of kids out for a joy ride . . . flat tire, empty gas tank. You name it. That's a nice girl. Wouldn't want to see her get hurt any more than the inevitable. Of course, you're not off the hook yet. There's still a couple of things that don't check out . . . that locket one. So don't jump bail or anything like that."

"Nothing like that," Johnny said wryly, and at the click on the other end of the receiver he slowly put down the one he held. His mother was standing in the doorway of his room waiting impatiently for him to be finished.

"What was that all about?" she said.

"I don't know," he said, "but I'm sure as hell going to find out."

"Bad or good?" his mother said as he flew into his room and began throwing on clothes.

"Chief Jones made it sound good. But I'll just have to let you know later. Sounds to me like Bibsy's gone off the deep end."

In his haste and confusion he forgot all about the job at Stone's. He went straight to the Michaels' house. But somebody had already got there beforehand. A coatless, excited-looking somebody with a pad and pencil in one hand and a tripod camera in the other. He was hammering earnestly on the Michaels' door, and if he heard Johnny drive up he didn't turn around to see who it was. Johnny sat in his car watching him for a few minutes, but when it became obvious that the door wasn't going to open, Johnny drove off. Maybe the coatless one could have enlightened him but right now the only enlightenment he wanted was from Bibsy, and he'd suddenly remembered about Stone's. But that was all he remembered. He hadn't the foggiest notion where to look for her. Not even on which floor. Cathy would know, of course. If he could just find lingerie. There was a big blackboard over beside the elevators that would give him this information, and it was as he made his way toward it that he spotted Bibsy. She was standing behind the cosmetic counter. She looked taller than he remembered and thinner and older. She was showing a heavyset, wrinkled woman a skin preparation, opening the jar, rubbing a little of the cream on the top of her hand.

"You see how easily it goes on," she was saying. "No grease."

"But five dollars . . ." The woman fingered her bag uncertainly. Johnny leaned against the far end of the counter pretending to study the various shades of lipstick on display.

"When you consider what they charge for a facial in a beauty parlor . . ."

"But my skin is so unresponsive . . ." Still she was opening the bag, groping for her change purse. And out of the corner of her eye Bibsy had seen him. Seen him and looked quickly away.

Finally the woman and her unresponsive skin departed, taking the cream, and Bibsy, smiling somewhat tremulously, said, "Can I interest you in our new shade? It's called . . ."

But he was in no mood for bantering. "I got a rather mystifying call from Chief Jones this morning," he said, keeping his voice down, out of earshot of whoever might be passing by. "What's it all about?"

"Didn't he tell you?" She looked at him, looked away, flushed. "You've got yourself an alibi. Didn't he tell you?"

"Just what is my alibi?"

"You were with me that night. All of that night." Her voice dropped to a whisper. "Until five in the morning."

"You told him that?"

For answer she nodded her head slowly, sagely, and for a moment let her eyes meet his. "And he believed me," she whispered, her eyes lighting, shining into his.

"Oh, no," Johnny groaned. "Look, Bibs . . ." But his throat felt tight, and he had to stop and clear it and besides he didn't know what to say, what not to say. The crazy little fool! What the hell did she have to go messing into this for! Weren't there already enough people hurting.

Everybody Adored Cara 151

And besides . . . "You can't do this, you know," he said. "I won't let you. It's ridiculous. And unnecessary. Just for your information I don't need an alibi. Was that what you were thinking? That you'd jump in and save me from the gallows? What the hell were you thinking?" If they'd been anywhere else he'd have made her look at him.

"I knew you'd be like this." She brushed a hand quickly, furtively to her eyes. "But I went ahead anyway. And now it's done."

"How done? Just how done is it? Who besides Link Jones?"

"My parents. The newspapers." Her chin lifted defiantly. "All the way done."

"Did you really think I was in that much trouble?"

"I didn't think anything. For once in my life I just felt."

"But you do see that I can't let it go on?"

"No." She looked at him now. "You've got to. It's too late. I've lied. To the police. They call it committing perjury and it's a crime. Chief Jones told me."

"Bibs." He reached over the counter, captured one of her hands in his. He no longer cared where they were. "Didn't you know that I loved Cara? Truly loved her? And still do."

"I knew. You told me yourself. The night you got potted."

"What did I tell you?"

"Not much. You wept for her and called me by her name."

He let go her hand then. There was nothing more he could do. Say. Except "Thank you." And feeling no gratitude, only a terrible impotent fury at himself, at the world, at her, it was no good.

She must have read some of this in his face for she said, "I did this as much for myself as for you. You must remember that. You must always remember that." She turned to greet a woman who wanted a perfume that would "stay with" her.

"Nothing stays with me," the woman said plaintively, "not even Patou."

Marny had been once more sent to "visit" the Browns, but she called that morning right after breakfast begging to come home, reducing Lindsey to silent helpless tears with her, "I'll promise not to get in the way and ask questions. Don't you even *miss* me?"

Dotty Brown dropped her off about eleven. Johnny had still not returned from his mysterious errand and Lindsey, distraught and restless, had chosen to polish the silver. Marny, true to her promise, would have scuttled off to her room but Lindsey, glad of company, gave her a cloth and a cream pitcher and invited her to help. Marny's chatter about the Browns' dog, about Lulu Brown's puppets, about her own project for the summer, a tree house in the maple by the back gate, were soothing. Reminding Lindsey that there was a world outside the nightmare world in which they lived of late.

And then Marny was saying: "Do you suppose Cara is allowed a cat in heaven?"

"I'm sure if she wanted one . . ."

"Oh, she wanted one. Maybe she's got Chicory."

"Who is Chicory?"

"Just a cat." For a moment she was pensive. Rubbing over and over the same place on the pitcher. "If I tell you something, you won't get mad?"

"Promise," Lindsey said absently.

"Well, now that I've had so long to think about it . . . but you see when they asked me I honestly, truly, cross my heart was sure, but now I'm not any more . . . I'm not sure it was Cara." Her words tumbled over each other in her haste to explain, to be understood. "When I saw somebody, a lady somebody, come out of Cara's house that night, I thought it was Cara. I mean, wouldn't anybody? So when they asked me that's what I told them. But they asked me so many times and made me think about it over and over and over, and now I'm not sure . . ."

"That often happens, dear, when we think too hard about anything."

"But if it had been Cara I would have seen her hair, wouldn't I?"

"In the dark?"

"There was a light somewhere. Enough so I knew it was a lady, and, and, and she didn't have on the turtledove dress."

"Should she have?" Lindsey smiled.

"I think so. That was the dress she had on in the afternoon, and it was by her bed all rumpled up when I, when the policemen were there . . ."

She faltered and rubbed her nose with her fist. "But anyhow, I didn't see her hair."

"What did you see?" Lindsey tried not to sound too interested. But she was. Any straw now . . .

"Just a lady with something white around her neck and around her middle."

"A collar? A belt?"

"Probably. Anyhow the turtledove dress didn't have a collar or a belt. Nothing but white turtledoves flying over the green. It was my favorite."

"Why do you think you didn't see Cara's hair?"

"I just didn't. It's what I always see first, and then Cara. I didn't see it that night. I thought it was Cara. So I didn't notice that I didn't see it, but I remember I didn't."

"Did you see any hair at all?"

"Just a head is all I saw. There probably was hair. Maybe it was black hair."

"Maybe Cara had on a hat."

"Maybe," Marny sighed, looking relieved. "Or a scarf. She never did wear a hat."

"May I have a word with you?" Johnny stood in the kitchen doorway. Lindsey tried to read in his expression what sort of tidings he brought but could not.

"Be right back," she told Marny who, eyes averted, was trying very hard 'not to get in the way.'

She went into the television room and Johnny, following her, closed the door and then to her consternation took his time. Found a cigarette in the desk drawer, lighted it, walked to the window, turned around. "I was right," he said. "Bibsy has gone off the deep end." But he was grinning, almost, halfway anyhow, and she took her cue from this.

"It's good news then?"

"Depends on how you look at it. I've got myself an ailbi. On the other hand, Bibsy has perjured herself."

"An alibi! Oh, Johnny, how wonderful! What is it? Good I hope. Solid good." She was almost crying with joy and Johnny, who'd been about to say something, thought better of it. His mouth snapped shut, and he flicked an imaginary ash from the end of his cigarette onto the rug.

"According to Bibsy," he said in a moment, "she was with me that night. We were together all night. Until five in the morning. Is that good?"

"Is it true?"

"Of course not."

"Then why?"

"The little fool has some idea of saving my neck. She . . ."

"Then let her!" Lindsey cried and then, shocked, shamed, she said. "Are you sure it isn't true? That you're not just trying to cover up for her?"

"Mother!" His voice was a slap designed to bring her to her senses. "Even if you don't know Bibsy any better than that, you don't think that I . . . ?"

"I don't know what I think any more," Lindsey moaned. "And worse, far worse, I don't even know what

I believe..." And then at the lost and stricken look on her son's face she rallied. "That's not really true, you know. I know what I *believe,* it's just how I *feel* that has got of hand." She smiled wanly. "Of course Bibsy mustn't be allowed to go through with this thing. But it would give us time, a little time, if for a little while you were in the clear..."

"Well, we've got that whether we want it or not. Bibsy has spilled the story to the papers and Link Jones seems convinced..."

"Yes, time," Lindsey murmured, "there are so many things, so many roads unexplored. But who's to do it, Johnny? Garfield is so sure that you are the one he's lost interest in any other possibility."

"He never had any interest..." Johnny said.

"I wish I knew how much faith to put in Marny..." Lindsey mused. "She says now she doesn't think it was Cara she saw coming out of the house that night. And I don't think she's trying to get attention. It really bothers her. She is beginning to develop a healthy respect for the truth, and she's afraid she was wrong."

"Now, Mother, I hate to prick your bubble, but Marny is feeling like the party's over and she'd only just begun to dance... Besides, who would listen to the vacillations of an eight-year-old child?"

The only one who would was at this moment harassing the staff of the Stoningham Inn with questions pertaining to the four days that Mrs. Helen Sumner had resided there.

It was difficult to know what to ask when he wasn't sure of what he was looking for, like a dog who digs for a bone whose shape and scent are unknown to him. He began with the maid whose duty it was to clean and tidy the third-floor rooms. She had been with the inn several years and yes, Mrs. Sumner had stayed there a number of times. Always in the same room which was a corner room and quite the nicest of the less expensive rooms at the inn. She wasn't much on tips the maid conceded, but then she wasn't any trouble either, neat and tidy and never asking extra favors. "Real quiet, too, not like some of these lonesome women that'll talk your ear off if you let 'em."

"Then you wouldn't say that Mrs. Sumner was particularly lonesome?"

"Oh, she was that all right, or at least she looked it to me, but one of those that kept herself to herself. Proud you might say."

"Did you notice anything different about her last time she was here?"

"Different?"

"Did she act any different? Seem nervous? Upset?"

"Not that I could see. The same quiet lady"—she cocked a prim brow—"minding her own business and me minding mine. Course she was sick one day, stayed in bed all morning. She was having a lot of dental work done; said it wore her out. And she looked it too."

"What day was that that she was sick?"

"How should I remember? One day's like another when you've work to do. Speaking of which . . ."

The desk clerk, a young man earning his way through night school, was less help. His job was undemanding and left him plenty of time to pore over the textbooks he kept on a shelf beside him. Clearly he took little interest in the people that passed before his desk each day.

He couldn't place any Mrs. Sumner until Tom pointed out that she'd had room thirty-six for several days only a little over a week ago.

"Oh, she was the one who was always asking if there were any messages. Felt sorry for her."

"Why?"

"There never were."

But sorry or not he couldn't remember what she looked

like or anything about her comings and goings. They were interrupted in this frustrating conversation several times by the telephone. The inn had only one or two outgoing lines, and it was the clerk's duty to take the calls and relay them to the operator. After a couple of these interruptions Tom noticed that whenever the clerk picked up the receiver he jotted the number given him on a huge blotter in front of him. The blotter was immersed in these doodlings, and the youth seeing him eyeing it speculatively, said, "I've got a memory like a sieve. Numbers especially."

"Do you always do this?"

"I told you. I hafta."

"Can I have a look?"

"Sure, sure . . ." Sullenly the youth got up, relinquishing his chair. "But what . . . ?"

"Nothing probably," Tom bent over the blotter. "How long have you had this same blotter?"

"About a month."

And then Tom saw the number he was looking for. The Merrill number. Laurel 2-2446. It was at the end of the blotter nearest him and undoubtedly represented one of the calls he'd made from the inn. And just how many had he made? He sat back on his haunches and shut his eyes. That first night and, and . . . Then that morning, yesterday, when Mrs. Merrill had cut him off short. And then last night to Cathy. That was all, wasn't it? Three calls was all. He opened his eyes.

"Do you have any system? I mean is there some place you start with a fresh blotter and . . ."

"At the top. Always at the top. And then . . ." He grinned rather sheepishly. "I kind of work down the sides. Right side first. Don't ask me why. Habit."

"So these numbers near the bottom," he touched a finger to the Merrill number, "are recent, and these others go back about a month."

"About that."

Tom took the vacated seat and began, slowly, methodically, to study the myriad numbers. He started with the bottom ones. He found the Merrill number again about an inch above the first one and then again to the left and down. He began again at the top. It was hard going. Some of the numbers ran into each other, others were so blotter-blurred he could scarcely make them out. He didn't really expect to find anything, but at least he now knew what he was looking for. He was looking for some connection between Mrs. Helen Sumner and her ex-husband. Unlike the clerk he did have a memory for numbers, and though he had only called the Sumner house once and that time from a downtown pay booth, he didn't need to looked it up. It too was a Laurel exchange. Laurel 2-4576. And there it was! And there again! He let his breath out in a whistle and pointed to the middle left hand side of the blotter.

"Can you say about when these calls were made? Take your time. It's important." He got up and stood back so the clerk could better study the area he'd indicated.

"Well, let's see." For the first time the youth appeared interested. "The way it goes is about four to five weeks for a blotter. And I don't hit around here until along about the third week maybe. Yep, I'd say that was about a week, two weeks ago." He straightened. "Now maybe you'll tell me what this is in the nature of . . ."

"I wish I knew," Tom said, grinning in spite of himself, "but I'll tell you one thing. If it's in the nature of what I think it is, I'll send you a bottle of scotch. Just one more thing, sonny. What hours are you on here?"

"Eleven A.M. until six P.M."

"And the night clerk, does he write down the calls, too?

"Not him. He's taking a correspondence course in accounting."

Tom started to call Cathy and tell her where he was going . . . her voice a good-luck piece to take with him on this crazy cavalier mission . . . but a look at his watch told him she'd probably be on her lunch hour. Just as well. If nothing came of it he'd not feel so much the fool . . . On the now familiar drive to Hastings he rehearsed his part. God knows he'd seen it in the movies and on television often enough. So probably had Helen Sumner. The smart guy who pretends to know all. Smooth, firm, a little contemptuous. "I happen to know, Mrs. Sumner, that you placed two calls to the Garfield Sumner home while you were in Stoningham. Your ex-husband was out of town. With whom did you wish to speak?" . . . "I happen to know Mrs. Sumner that you were so upset the morning after Cara Sumner was murdered that you took to your bed . . ." "I'm as sure as I'm standing here, Mrs. Sumner, that you know something that you aren't telling. Who are you trying to protect? And now that they've booked the Merrill boy, why do you think you must protect anyone?"

And come to think of it just who was she trying to protect? Her ex-husband? And if so, why? And from what? And also just what was to prevent Mrs. Sumner from laughing in his face. . . . "Those calls? Why, Garfield was late with his monthly check. It often takes a little prodding. I didn't know he was out of town." Or, "I've not the slightest idea what you're talking about. What calls? It must have been someone else." The closer he got to Hastings the more uncertain he felt. There was nothing to go on really but the sure knowledge that she'd lied to him and got herself plastered in the process.

The white house with the green shutters looked just as it had when he'd left it the day before. The black coupe with the whitewall tires was still parked in the drive. The whole scene had a static look as though nothing had happened or were ever going to happen. The breathless summer air in which no breeze stirred to bring grass or tree alive contributed to this sensation of time held motionless. Before getting out of the car Tom looked about for the dog. But he was nowhere in sight, and cautiously Tom walked up the path to the closed front door. Before he reached the door he heard the dog whimper inside. It startled him far more than the expected growl or bark would have done. It was a plaintive sound and continuous, like the crying of a child. He could find no bell and was about to knock when suddenly the dog's head appeared at one of the glass panels that ran up either side of the entranceway. There was none of yesterday's fierceness in the animal face that peered up at him through the glass. The ears lay flat and smooth against his massive head and in his eyes there was a look of pleading. As they eyed each other, man and dog, the whimpering persisted on a more querulous note, and all at once the dog leaped up and scratched at the glass panel with both forepaws. Tom's first thought was that the dog simply wanted out, but having left his claw marks on the glass he turned abruptly and disappeared. Tom cupped his hands about his eyes and looked through the pane after him. Halfway down the hall the dog stopped and looked back over his shoulder, whimpered, turned, took a few more steps, turned, looked back at Tom and whimpered again. Tom knocked and the dog stopped, sat down, his back to Tom, facing what might have been the closed kitchen door. Now Tom pounded on the front door with both fists, but his only answer was the distressed whimper of the dog inside. Running to the back of the house Tom tried the back door, but it too was locked. He picked up a rake that was leaning against the back steps and returning to the front of the house, crashed the wooden handle of the rake through the panel nearest the door's latch. It was simple then to reach in and unbolt the lock. And as he did so he felt the dog's warm tongue brush the back of his hand.

Once inside it took a moment to orient himself after the brightness of the sun outside, but the dog was impatient. The whimpering had stopped and now he panted. His great tongue lolling wearily from the side of his jaw, he paced circles around his rescuer.

Everybody Adored Cara 161

"What is it, old boy?" He glanced briefly into the room where Mrs. Sumner had "entertained" him the day before, but there was nothing there and following the dog's earlier hint he strode down the hall and opened the door at the end of it. It opened into the kitchen all right And on the kitchen floor clad in pajamas and robe across which oozed and spread the bright, harsh stain of blood, lay Helen Sumner. His thumb and forefinger placed against her wrist told him that she still lived. The dog, his duty done, collapsed in a corner where, nose on paws, he followed Tom with hopeful, tired eyes.

It took, it seemed to Tom, an agonizingly long time to find the telephone. It was in an alcove underneath the stairs, not the first place one would look. Dialing the operator he hoped that Hastings was as small at it appeared and that the operator was the nosy sort who would know all about everyone and just whom to call for what. She gave him the number of a Dr. Rayburn who might or might not be Mrs. Sumner's doctor, but was, she'd heard, always available for house calls.

"This isn't a house call," he all but shouted, "this is an emergency. The woman has been shot."

"Goodness," breathed the operator. "Then you'll probably be wanting the police too, won't you?"

"Yeah, yeah, how about you calling them while I call the doctor?"

"I'll have to have your name and . . ."

"Ridley, Tom Ridley." He slammed down the receiver, disconnecting them. Picking it up he dialed the number she'd given him. Dr. Rayburn, a woman's voice informed him, was busy. Would he like to leave a message? No, he damned well wouldn't. He'd like to speak to the doctor at once.

It seemed to him when he returned to the kitchen that it had been hours since he left it, but in reality, as the kitchen clock testified, it had only been about ten minutes. He felt that there should be something he could do for the unconscious woman, but he knew better than to try. And he needed these few minutes before the doctor and police got there to look around. The pistol, a .22 automatic which he had not seen until now, lay beneath the kitchen table a bare few inches from her outstretched hand. The kitchen was spotlessly clean, not even a soiled glass in sight. He opened and shut a couple of cupboard doors, came upon one that was locked. It was probably here that she kept the wine she drank. He moved on into the dining room. On the dining-room table was a Stoningham newspaper open to a page containing, among other things, the continuation from page one of the latest findings in the Blue Chiffon Murder, the story of Johnny Merrill's arrest. Beside it was notepaper and pen and for a moment Tom thought this might be the suicide note, but the paper, a pale blue linen, was blank. Whatever Helen Sumner had meant to write she had apparently thought better of it. On the floor next to the chair was an empty glass. He picked it up. Sniffed it. But if there had ever been anything stronger than water in it, it was no longer discernible.

He was halfway up the stairs on his way to the bedrooms when there was a pounding on the front door. He turned and ran down the steps, calling that the door was open. The door opened just before he reached it, but it was not the doctor who strode in, looking at him and through him as though he weren't there. It was Garfield Sumner, and he wanted to know where Helen was. Dumfounded, Tom jerked his thumb in the direction of the kitchen.

"She's hurt," Tom said. "The doctor ought to be here any minute." But Garfield wasn't listening. He disappeared through the kitchen door, and in a moment Tom followed after him. He was standing beside the inert form staring down at it with a look of angry puzzlement.

"What happened?" He addressed Tom, still seeming hardly to acknowledge his presence. "Is she dead?"

"No, she's not dead."

Everybody Adored Cara

"Shot?"

For answer Tom directed his glance to the pistol which still remained untouched beneath the kitchen table. "It looks as though it was something she did herself, though it's possible that . . ."

"See here," Garfield interrupted, "what are *you* doing here?"

"I might ask you the same."

"She called me. But what business is this of . . . ah, the doctor." He broke off and went out into the hall to greet Dr. Rayburn. His voice explaining his presence there could be quite plainly heard by Tom who sat on the counter edge nervously drumming his feet . . . "Called last night. All in a swivet about the Merrill boy, didn't make much sense. Thought it over and this morning . . ." They came into the room now, the doctor, a florid, hefty man, hurrying ahead oblivious of Garfield's voice trailing in his wake . . . "decided I'd better take a run down. Never been here before in my life . . ." The doctor bent over Helen Sumner; folding back her robe, he began quickly, deftly, to unfasten her pajamas. Tom, out of deference, turned away.

"We'll need an ambulance," the doctor said. "The number is 223. Will someone . . ." But Tom was already on his feet.

"Do you think she'll live?" Garfield was saying in a voice that contained, it seemed to Tom, little more than annoyance. The doctor, busy with sponges, with tweezers, with a hypodermic needle, did not reply.

Being interrogated by the police was a new experience for Tom. However, the Hastings police, the two of them to be exact, were hardly a formidable pair. A Mutt and Jeff combination. The tall one asked most of the questions, the short one being more interested in the contents of Helen Sumner's bookcase. Kept his back to them.

"Came out here to talk to the lady about the Blue Chiffon case, eh?" Tall One said. "Think she knew something about it?"

"I was hoping that was all."

"And what do you think now?"

"What do *you* think? It's pretty obvious she had something on her mind."

"With a woman it could be anything. So you knock and when nobody answers, you break in?"

"It was the dog that made me think something was wrong. The way he acted. He just about told me."

"So you and the dog have a talk and you break in!"

"And a lucky thing I did, wouldn't you say?"

"All depends," Tall One said judiciously.

"In that case, why can't we let all this wait until we see . . ."

"See what?"

"If she's going to live."

"She sure was deep," Short One said, turning away from the bookshelves with a shrug. "Psychiatry, philosophy, and the likes."

Helen Sumner was still alive late that afternoon when Tom drove back to Stoningham. Alive but not conscious. He turned on the car radio and got the six o'clock news out of Stoningham, but it was a national hookup and not concerned with anything local. Though he was sure the story wouldn't have broken in time for the afternoon papers, he stopped a few miles out of Stoningham and bought a paper anyway.

It was then that he first learned that Johnny had got himself an alibi. He wasn't at all sure there was any truth in the Michael girl's story . . . she didn't look the type for an all-night joy ride, nor could he buy Johnny Merrill as a cold-blooded seducer of married women *and* virgins . . . but still for the present it was an alibi, and it might prove

Everybody Adored Cara 165

all that was needed to jolt Garfield into a few second thoughts on the murder of his wife.

He would give his eyeteeth to know just what had transpired on the telephone between Sumner and Helen Sumner the night before, but he was too tired now to figure how to go about finding out. For the immediate present all he wanted was a cool shower and to hear the excitement in Cathy's voice when he told her that he had possibly saved the life that day of the one person who who could help Johnny.

He called her as soon as he got to his room. But there was no excitement in her voice. Helen Sumner's attempted suicide appeared to her as but one more tragedy in a series of tragedies, none of them having any rhyme or reason. The only time she betrayed any emotion was when he asked if he might see her later that evening. Her "Oh yes" was young and breathless and what he had been waiting for.

Sumner had no intention of going to Hastings to check on the telephone call from his former wife until the next morning when Link Jones told him that Johnny had an alibi. Until then he'd attached little or no importance to the near hysterical call except to realize that Helen was drinking too much and that if he weren't beyond feeling anything, he would feel sorry for her.

She had never called him before. In fact he couldn't remember that he'd heard her voice since that day years ago when she'd finally agreed to a divorce. He had forgotten how very delicate and precise her voice was. Blurred by the effects of whatever it was she was drinking last night, it had had the singsong lightness of music. She began by berating him for someone she kept referring to in the manner of one of Tennessee Williams' characters, as a "gentleman caller." This person she said had made a nuisance of himself and would Garfield see to it that in the future he stayed away. Garfield, having no idea of what or whom she spoke and anxious to have the conversation terminated, agreed to do his best. This instead of silencing her brought forth a storm of angry tears. "So it *was* you sent him here to pry and ask questions! Haven't you done enough, you and your precious Cara . . ." Then there was a lot more that was garbled in which he made out the words "deceive" and "destroy" and then silence. A silence so prolonged that he was on the point of hanging up when she said quite slowly, quite distinctly, "How old is Johnny Merrill now?"

"Nineteen, twenty. Old enough!"

"Still it seems too bad . . ."

"For Christ's sake, Helen, what are you driving at? What did you call to say?"

"I'm not quite sure any more," she said, and he heard the soft final click of the receiver going down at the other end of the line.

So Helen was drinking too much and still bitter about the divorce. That's how he wrote it off. And then first thing the next morning Link got to him with the alibi story. Not that he believed it. Just something the boy had trumped up to save his neck, but still there it was, an alibi. "Gotta face facts. Know what?" Link had said. "I think you wanted that boy hung, determined to get him hung the minute you heard your wife was dead. And I don't blame you. But maybe in the heat of it you got carried away. Believed what you wanted to believe."

He didn't entirely believe that either, but it did make a dent, and the more he thought about Helen's call the more uneasy he became. For instance, who was this mysterious gentleman caller that she thought he'd sent to harass her? Johnny Merrill looking for something, hoping for something . . . but why Helen? And so he'd driven to Hastings that morning to find Helen half-dead. His first reaction was one of frustration. He'd come all this way to talk to Helen and now she wasn't talking to anyone. He realized that this was hardly a decent emotion to entertain at such a moment, but he couldn't help it. It was all too reminiscent of the times he'd come home prepared to "take the bull by the horns" and not just ask but demand a divorce, only to find she was going out to a meeting or had asked people in for the evening. It was only when the police came that he began to wonder why Helen would want to do away with herself.

Garfield followed the ambulance into town to a small brick edifice that called itself the Hastings Infirmary but the stretcher, bearing Helen, disappeared behind doors marked Surgery, and as there seemed nothing further to do, he drove back to Stoningham.

The windows of the Merrill house next door were all open to receive the twilight cool, and as he walked up the path to his own front door he could hear now and then the sound of voices, the clatter of pots and pans being readied for the cooking of the evening meal. In contrast his house seemed silent, empty, and infinitely forlorn. But where else? He didn't enjoy his club any more where he was now treated with singular deference if not downright pity. When this was all over he would move, of course, but now there was nothing for it but to march, head up, a soldier facing unknown enemies, to his own front door. He was more relieved than startled by a brash masculine voice assailing him from the shadowed bench underneath the maple tree beside the porch.

"May I have a word with you, Mr. Sumner? I'm from the *Stoningham Evening Press and Standard*." The man emerged from the shadows, pad and pencil in hand. "What is your reaction to the new angle on the Blue Chiffon case?"

"New angle?"

"Yeah, looks like Merrill's in the clear. What's your reaction?"

Garfield, his hand on the front door knob, tried to summon the anger that had become second nature, reflex almost, but all he felt was an enormous weariness that seemed to start in his head. "What makes you so sure he's in the clear?" he said, but there was no bite to it.

"The alibi. The girl . . ."

"Oh, that," Garfield said and turned and walked into the house, closing and bolting the door behind him.

He went immediately upstairs, showered and got into bed, but he didn't sleep. He didn't really expect to. Thoughts, emotions, memories crowded in on him. First Cara and now Helen. Just how far could you stretch coincidence? Far enough to write off a murder and an attempted suicide in the space of a week? Even he could not, much as he wished to. And so painfully, cautiously he approached the possibility that they were related. It wasn't an easy thing for him to do. It meant confronting once more a time that he didn't like to remember. It meant thinking about Helen. About their marriage. And he wasn't sure where any of it would lead. He was half-tempted to take a sleeping pill and forget the whole thing . . . call off the bloodhounds . . . and he probably would have except for a feeling in his bones that the day was not yet finished, that he still waited for something to happen.

He had married Helen without love. Was that, then, the beginning? It hadn't been deliberate. He simply hadn't known. At that time he'd never experienced a passionate involvement, a total involvement with a woman. He still dreamed of one. He met Helen at the wedding of a friend. She was handsome in a conventional way, the only child of elderly parents she had, like himself, had a strict and proper upbringing.

They knew many of the same people or at least people who knew the same people and had all their lives breathed much the same rarified, upper-echelon air. They had much in common including the fact that they were both secretly beginning to be a little anxious about finding a mate. Helen probably more intensely anxious than he ever guessed. For two years he squired her here and there and now and then imagined himself in love, and when his imagination failed to take hold, began to suspect that he expected far too much of the emotion, that it had been vastly overrated. One rainy night shortly after Helen's father died, touched by her tight-lipped grief, moved by her mute appeal to him for comfort, he asked her to marry him.

Theirs was not an unhappy marriage from her standpoint. Perhaps he should have let her know sooner that what for her was complete fulfillment—a pleasant home, social position, a courteous husband who made few demands on her, was for him a slow death. But he didn't let her know, and then he met Cara. Helen was shocked, outraged, and deeply frightened by his request for a divorce. She stormed and raged and wept for days after that first request. He'd had no idea she was capable of such passion, and he determined then and there not to tell her about Cara. Was that too a sin? The reason he'd given himself at the time was that he saw no point in wounding Helen further, and perhaps that had been a part of it. Now, in all honesty, he acknowledged that he'd also feared she might, if she knew, never have set him free. As it was it took an interminable time to persuade her. He finally convinced her that if she did not leave him he would leave her. This humiliation she couldn't face, so she left.

She still didn't instigate proceedings until she was entirely convinced that he would never change and found that divorced from him she would receive more income than she did merely living apart from him. Once the proceedings were underway she maintained a calm and reasonable exterior. Her story was that they'd "grown bored with each other," that the divorce was merely an "experiment." He was much too involved with his own affairs to pay any attention to her pitiful attempts at face-saving. And could only now at this moment, the memory of her crumpled on the kitchen floor at Hastings fresh in his mind, see how his marriage to Cara, the day after the divorce became final, must have affected her. The realization brought with it no twinge of conscience nor even honest compassion, for he knew in spite of all and everything he would do the same thing over again had he the chance. He had learned nothing, gained nothing, and therein he recognized the enormity of the tragedy that had befallen him . . . and Cara . . . and perhaps Helen too.

It was almost nine when the call came. And the moment the operator said "Hastings Infirmary calling Mr. Garfield Sumner," he knew that this was what he'd been waiting for and knew too, in a terrible moment of self-revelation, that he hoped they were going to tell him that Helen was dead. But they didn't. They said that she had regained consciousness but was very agitated and wanted to see him. They said they thought it important that he come. They gave him no choice.

When he walked into the hospital room and looked down on the pale anguished face on the pillow, he tried to imagine it was the face of Johnny Merrill lying there so that he could feel the way he should feel about Cara's murderer, but it was still Helen's eyes that stared back at him, dark with pain, Helen's long-fingered hand that indicated the chair on the other side of the bed where she wished him to sit.

"You look as though I don't need to tell you anything, as though already you . . ." she said and turned her face toward the ceiling and closed her eyes. "When did you know?"

"Tonight. Maybe sooner. I'm not sure."

"I didn't mean to. I didn't even know that she was dead until I read it in the papers. I wanted to be sure you knew that before I told anyone else. I wanted to be sure you knew I didn't mean to . . ."

A nurse came and stuck a thermometer in her mouth,

took it out. "You mustn't stay too long. Only fifteen minutes Dr. Rayburn said."

"Do you want to begin at the beginning?" Garfield said, when the nurse had gone.

"I'm not sure I know where the beginning is . . . our marriage, the divorce, your remarriage, my drinking, it could be anywhere . . ."

"I'm afraid there isn't time for that; fifteen minutes the nurse said."

"You see, that morning I called your office first. I—I needed some money: a loan. They didn't tell me you were out of town, only that you weren't going to be in that day. So I thought I might reach you at home. But your wife answered the telephone. I hated her, you know," she said without emotion. "I'd never seen her, but I hated her." She paused, and for a moment he was afraid she was too tired to go on. "She didn't seem to know it. She was very pleasant, cordial even. She said it was too bad we'd never met; she invited me to come for a drink that afternoon. I refused. But after I'd hung up I realized she hadn't the slightest idea how I felt about her, or of what she'd done to me. I decided that she should know, that it was only fair . . . that she should suffer *something*. So I called her back but by then she'd made other plans for that hour, and she suggested I come later, after dinner. I can't describe how I felt all that day—exhilarated is hardly the word, and you'd have to know how much I'd suffered with this hate all bottled up inside."

"Cara never knew she'd hurt you or rather that I'd hurt you," Garfield interrupted. "I never told her. She thought we were getting a divorce when I met her, that you wanted it as much as I."

"It is cruel of you to tell me this now."

"So you went to meet Cara and told her off . . ."

"The point is I didn't. I went to the house, but I never got a chance to say anything I meant to say, anything I wanted to say, had wanted to say for years. She never let me." She broke off, shut her eyes, and Garfield appalled watched the tears of self pity that ran from the closed lids.

"How did she prevent you?"

"I don't really know. At first it was the hair and the eyes and her beautiful figure. I saw what had happened to you, what could happen to any man if she wanted it to. Then she began talking, about everything and nothing, radiating charm, drawing me into the room offering coffee, a brandy. I finally managed to say that I hadn't come to make friends with her, but she didn't seem to hear me. Somehow she knew I'd been to school in Washington and apparently she'd lived there for a while. She started talking about that, asking me questions. I felt all purpose slipping away from me, a paralyzing unbearable lassitude settling over me. Right in the middle of something she was saying, I leaped up and fled the place . . ." Exhausted she stopped, and this time Garfield felt it would be well not to prod her, let her get her second wind. The waiting was interminable. He looked at his watch. In another few minutes the nurse would be shooing him out. But he said nothing.

"If only I'd let it go at that." Her voice was very low, and he had to bend close to the bed to hear. "Of late I've found whiskey very soothing. When I got back to my room I had a drink. But it didn't soothe me, quite the opposite, so I had another. It made me strong again, sure of myself, and I knew I must go back, had to go back, and tell her what she'd done to me. Puncture some of that innocent complacency. Let her know that she lived on another woman's happiness. Do you understand? I had that to do!"

"And so you went back . . ."

"Yes, yes, I went back and there was still a light on, one downstairs, one upstairs . . . if there only hadn't been a light on . . ."

"Cara always left lights on at night. She feared the dark."

"I knocked on the front door, and when no one came, I went around to the back door. It wasn't locked, but I think if it had been I'd have broken in somehow. Once inside I called her name even though it tasted like poison on my tongue. When she didn't answer I went upstairs to the room where the light burned. It was her room. She was in bed, her eyes closed. I spoke her name again louder but she didn't stir, and then I saw the sleeping pills beside the bed and knew I'd have trouble waking her, but I was beyond caring about that. All I cared was that she *hear* me. I went close to the bed and shook her, her hand moved a little but that was all. She had to wake up. I told her so over and over. I think by then I was crying with frustration and defeat. There was a scarf beside the bed. I wrapped it about her neck and pulled at the ends. They say cut a person's wind off and they'll wake right up. There was a moment when she seemed to try to rouse herself, to struggle against sleep, and I let the scarf go, but she never opened her eyes. Suddenly I was frightened. I staggered back from the bed still crying at her to wake up, and then I turned and ran down the stairs and away. I don't know what I thought. I didn't think she was dead. I don't remember much about getting back to the inn or to my room. I remember looking in my mirror. I remember thinking 'Why Helen, you wouldn't hurt a flea! Everyone knows that!'"

"Time's up," the nurse said from the doorway and though her voice was cheerful enough the pale exhausted face on the pillow gave the pronouncement a prophetic ring. Garfield got up and for a moment let his hand rest on Helen's where it lay limp and cold against the coverlet but her eyes were closed and if she was aware of this gesture of compassion, of forgiveness she gave no sign.

Anyway from that lofty pinnacle could he offer forgiveness? She had committed the visible wrong but by what terrible series of invisible wrongs on his part had she been brought to this dark reckoning?

A light burned on the porch of the Michaels' house on Valence Street and another one upstairs in the room where Bibsy sat cross-legged on her bed writing in her diary. She was wearing candy-striped pajamas, and her hair was braided neatly into pigtails for the night. With her flat chest and tear-smudged face, she looked much too young to be writing anything at all.

"*He called tonight,*" she wrote, "*but I wouldn't see him. I don't ever want to see him again until . . .*" She thought about this a moment, scowling intently, shook her head, made a dash and started a new sentence. "*The thing nobody seems to realize is that he loved her, that there wasn't anything small or sordid about it.*

"*I don't feel as changed as I thought I'd feel. I still mind what people are thinking, the girls at the store, the way Dad looks at me, Mother crying* all *the time, but at least she went bowling with Dad tonight. First time in ages. Said she had to get her mind off her troubles. That's me. But I liked the way she took Dad's arm going down the steps.*

"*Tomorrow I think I'll go to India. There are scads of books on India at the library. I like the clothes the Indian women wear and the gardens. I think instead of just putting pins in the map I'll keep a journal. 'My Trip Through India.' It will make it more real and help to pass the time.*" She sighed, closed the diary, blew her nose once, hard, and turned off the light.

To Cathy the lake cottage in the moonlight appeared secretive and alert. "Like someone afraid to fall asleep for fear they might give something away," she said.

"Or miss something," Tom said.

They sat on the end of the dock, their bare feet ankle-deep in the water. They'd had dinner at the inn, hashing over the case until they were both weary of the subject. Afterward Cathy suggested they drive to the lake. "To cool off" was what she said. Actually the lake was her favorite place in all the world, and she wanted to show it to him. Strange this compulsion to share everything, as new and as inexplicable as love itself.

"That's where we came in," Cathy mused.

"Where?" He wasn't really following. He was soaking in the night, the stillness of water and trees and the sound of her voice weaving through the stillness.

"The fear of missing something, remember? When you first cross-examined me about Cara."

"I remember."

"I was afraid you'd think me terribly . . ." She paused, groping for the word . . . "I don't think you're really listening. What are you thinking about?"

"Nothing really. That's the joy of it."

"Of what?"

"Of being with you. I feel perfectly at home."

Her feet gave the water an angry splash. "I can't say I feel the same about you!"

"You will."

"When?"

"Now. In a minute." He turned and took her face in his hands and looked at her searchingly and long before he kissed her.

It was after one when Lindsey saw the headlights of a car sweep into the Sumner drive. She and Frank and Johnny were sitting at the kitchen table drinking coffee and arguing. There was no fear of their voices carrying as they spoke quietly and without rancor. Frank and Johnny were trying to explain to her why they could not accept the gift of Bibsy's alibi. The argument had been going on for hours, and Lindsey knew now it was a losing battle, that woman's heart and man's honor are irreconcilable, but even in defeat there was a certain pleasure to be had from hearing them, father and son, aligned together, their male logic pitted against her woman's will. Father and son in manly accord.

She had paid little attention to the car lights next door except to wonder what Garfield was doing out so late. But when she heard the front door, left unlocked for Cathy, open and close, heard the heavy, slow footsteps coming down the hall she knew it would be Garfield, and her heart leaped in apprehension. Yet when he stood all at once framed in the kitchen doorway, the garish kitchen light shining down on his haggard face, she was no longer afraid. Her thought, her first fleeting thought, before he spoke, was that Johnny was right. It was Garfield who had killed Cara. It was, it seemed to her, written all over him.